THE QUEST

FOUR FAE FOR THE PRINCESS
BOOK TWO

SADIE WATERS

For Ms. Sherry

CONTENTS

1

THE JOURNEY BEGINS

The moment we set out for Oceana, there's a palpable tension in the air. I can feel it coiling around us like a tight, invisible thread, threatening to choke me. I wonder if the others can feel it as well. Surely, they don't all have the weight of grief so heavy on their chests, threatening to crush them.

It took all the strength I have to leave my family in such a vulnerable state, knowing that war is inevitable. When I erected the barrier in the castle to seal them off from the rest of the world, I wasn't sure if it would last. We've not even been gone an hour, and I can't say for sure that the barrier is even still up.

I can't worry too much about it at present, though. My mind needs to stay sharp. The journey ahead is dangerous at best–and deadly at worst. It will define not only our fates but the future of Altinna itself. Most importantly, if we don't complete it, Mother will die.

My four Ones walk with me, surrounding me in a square formation. Akin leads to my left, close enough that he can push me out of harm's way if the moment strikes. Of all the men here, he's the only

1

one I truly know. The only one I truly love. When all this began, I'd hoped he was my only One, but it seems the fates had other ideas.

Permiton, the royal advisor who came to Altinna from Ambrosia is to my right. He's wise, of course, the way all royal advisors are. But he's also somewhat cold, calculated, cerebral to a fault. I don't know what to make of him yet, but I try to give him grace. He makes my magic stronger, and that's the best I can ask for at this point.

Brook and River fall back on either side of me. Brothers, they're the disowned princes from a now warring country. River clearly doesn't know how to follow behind, used to always being up front, the center of attention. Even though he's hardly in my line of sight, I can feel his disgust at his position. He and Akin don't get along at all. He and I don't get along much, either, but at this moment, it's Akin he resents for insisting to be at the front of our traveling party.

Brook is clearly more comfortable in his place, willing to stand behind in support. I still don't know him as well as I would like, but there's a gentleness to him. There's also a part of me that wants to defend him, to speak up for him when others talk over him. He's kind and humble, something his brother could use a lot more of.

The five of us move forward together, a coordinated unit. I need all of them to strengthen my magic, but there could be more, I think. At least with Akin and Brook. I already deeply love the man who's stood by my side for years and protected me. And I know that I could easily grow to love Brook. River and Permiton are unknowns, though. How am I supposed to spend the rest of my life with two men I don't trust? As we leave my kingdom, these are the thoughts that consume me.

We haven't gone far before Permiton, with his ever-calculated demeanor, speaks up. "We'll need to disguise ourselves," he tells us in his steady, almost monotonous voice.

I glance at him, puzzled, voicing my confusion.

"Disguise ourselves? Why?"

He sighs heavily and pinches the bridge of his nose as if my words have deeply annoyed him. As if the answer should be obvious.

"River and Brook have been disowned," he answers slowly.

"Oceana has declared war on Altinna. The moment we set foot on Oceanean soil, we will all be their enemy. If they recognize any of us, we'll be arrested. Or worse. We'll have to blend in."

"Blend in how, exactly?" Brook chimes in from behind me.

River groans, throwing his head back dramatically. "You expect us to dress as peasants, don't you?" he asks rudely. "I've been with you people for a few hours, and already you're making me sink far below my standards."

I roll my eyes at him, but Permiton's expression remains impassive. "This isn't a joke, River," he says in a calm, yet demanding, tone. "You know as well as I do that it's necessary."

River mutters something under his breath about his "refined tastes," but eventually, he relents, albeit begrudgingly, as we begin to exchange our royal attire for simple, worn traveling clothes. Akin, ever practical, dons his disguise without a word of complaint, his face set in quiet determination. Brook follows suit, though with less visible enthusiasm.

I try to suppress my amusement at River's clear discomfort as he fumbles with the coarse fabric of his peasant shirt. He wrinkles his nose in distaste, and I swear I hear him grumble, "Smells like dirt and misery."

Despite the tension between us, I can't help but find his dramatic nature amusing. I know better than to say anything that might provoke him, though. River's pride is as fragile as glass, and I'm not looking to get into a fight this early in the journey. We still have such a long way left to go.

We travel by day, the rough terrain unforgiving and difficult to navigate. The ground beneath us is uneven, the path winding through dense forests and rocky slopes, making it impossible to walk with any sense of comfort. As night begins to fall, we're all exhausted, and the grumbling gets worse. Specifically River's, of course.

"Why can't we just find an inn?" he grumbles. "I have plenty of gold with me. Maybe I'll even find a nice stable room for you, Akin," he chides, though Akin pays him no mind.

"Don't be dense, River," Brooks chastises. "We're fugitives now. We can't just go to an inn."

"Your brother is correct," Permiton agrees. "We'd do best to find a safe place in the woods to settle down."

We walk a little ways further through the dense forest until Akin finds a clearing of trees off the beaten path. We all settle on the rough ground, spreading out our thin blankets and attempting to get some sleep beneath the stars, though one of us has to be on guard at all times. The men are taking turns, all of them but River agreeing that I need to rest.

River complains, of course. Constantly. "I can't believe I'm expected to sleep on the ground like some kind of wild animal," he groans, adjusting his blanket for the tenth time.

Akin, who has been the picture of patience throughout the day, finally snaps. He sits up and shoots River a dark look.

"Suck it up, Prince," he growls. "We're all exhausted, so pretend for one moment that other people matter besides you."

River glares at him, but something in Akin's tone must strike a chord because he doesn't say anything else for the rest of the night. In fact, he offers to take the second watch after Permiton.

When morning comes, the journey continues. We travel through more remote, uninhabited areas, keeping to the edges of villages to avoid detection. Whenever we need supplies, Akin volunteers to go into the villages alone, using his experience and military training to keep a low profile. It's always a relief when he returns, supplies in hand.

Unfortunately, River is never satisfied with what he brings. "Is this really the best food you could find?" he complains, inspecting the meager provisions Akin brought back one afternoon, dried meat, bread that's more rock than dough, and a few root vegetables.

Akin's jaw tightens. "It's what they had. If you'd prefer to starve, that's your choice."

River tosses the dried meat back onto the pile with an exaggerated look of disgust. "It's practically inedible."

"If you want something better," Akin snaps, his patience clearly worn thin, "you're welcome to go into the village yourself and see how far you get with your princely airs."

River narrows his eyes, but he doesn't respond. He knows Akin is right. None of us can afford to draw attention to ourselves, least of all River and Brook. Despite his complaints, River eats the food, though not without making sure everyone knows how displeased he is.

We continue like this for several days, the rhythm of travel becoming almost monotonous. The nights are cold, the ground unforgiving, but we press on, knowing we have no other choice. Despite the tension and River's constant grumbling, we remain focused on our goal to find Bright Waters and save my mother.

Finally, after days of travel, we reach the border of Oceana, and with it, the Oceanean barrier.

The sight of it takes my breath away. It's not like the magical barrier surrounding Altinna, invisible yet ever-present. The Oceanean barrier is a vast, deep body of water, stretching as far as the eye can see, glimmering under the sunlight like a sheet of polished glass. The water is impossibly calm, as though no ripple or wave has ever disturbed its surface.

River's eyes light up as soon as he sees it. He's not even trying to mask his excitement.

"Civilization, finally," he says with a satisfied sigh. "And we finally get a break from walking."

I look between River and Brook, not quite understanding. River grins, the first genuine smile I've seen from him in days.

"You see, Princess," he says haughtily, seeing my confusion, "the Oceaneans have enchanted the large narwhals to pull ferries across the water. Beautiful, luxurious ferries. Just wait; you'll see."

He strides forward confidently, extending his hand over the water. For a moment, nothing happens. River's grin falters slightly, but he doesn't let it show. He waves his hand again, muttering a few words under his breath. Still nothing.

Brook frowns, stepping forward. "Maybe you're doing it wrong. Let me try."

River glares at him but steps aside. Brook approaches the water and lifts his hand, concentrating. I watch as the surface of the water remains still, unmoving, as though mocking their efforts. Brook frowns and tries again. Nothing's happening.

They exchange confused glances, and I can see the growing unease on their faces. River's confidence is fading fast, and Brook looks equally concerned.

"What's going on?" I ask, my heart sinking. "What's supposed to happen?"

Permiton, who has been standing off to the side, observing in his usual quiet manner, steps forward. His gaze shifts, as though he's seeing something the rest of us can't, and a grimace crosses his face.

"You've been denied entry to Oceana," he says quietly, his voice heavy with certainty. "Permanently."

River whirls around to face him, his eyes wide with disbelief. "What? That's impossible!"

"No," Permiton says, shaking his head. "Not impossible. Your father, the king, has barred you both from ever returning to the kingdom. Your water magic, strong as it might be, will never summon the narwhals while he's alive."

Brook's face pales, and River's expression darkens with rage.

"This is absurd," River mutters, his fists clenched. "I'm the Crown Prince of Oceana. He can't just—"

"He can," Permiton interrupts calmly. "And he has."

For a moment, we all stand there in silence, the weight of Permiton's words sinking in. If River and Brook can't summon the narwhals, how will we ever cross the barrier? How will we reach Bright Waters?

Brook sighs heavily and sinks onto the ground, the weight of his decision suddenly weighing on him. My heart aches for what he's given up for this, for me. Perhaps I would feel as sad for River if he showed an ounce of humanity. Either way, we're all stuck. We can't have come this far just to come this far.

I glance at the expanse of water before us, my mind racing.

"What are we supposed to do now?" I ask, turning to Permiton.

He gives me a small, enigmatic smile, the kind that suggests he knows more than he's letting on. "Wait and see," he says cryptically.

2

OBSTACLES

We wait by the water's edge, the air thick with unease. Brook seems weighted down with the reality of being banished from his kingdom. River, on the other hand, is incensed, muttering to himself about how unfair this all is.

Akin is restless, eager to be moving. He tells us multiple times that he doesn't like how exposed we are and thinks we should go back to the forest for cover until we figure out our next move. Permiton keeps telling him that our help will come soon.

The vast body of water in front of us stretches endlessly, the deep blue surface unnaturally still. It reflects the gray sky above, creating an almost eerie mirror-like effect. I'm trying to stay calm, to trust in Permiton, but his cryptic reassurances aren't doing much to ease my anxiety.

"Permiton," I finally say, unable to keep my doubts to myself any longer "are you sure about this?"

He stands a little apart from the rest of us, his eyes scanning the horizon as if waiting for something only he can see. When I speak, he doesn't turn, but I can see his shoulders tense slightly.

"I'm certain," he says, his voice even. "But patience is necessary. From all of us."

He turns to Akin to give him a meaningful look, and Akin stands still, glowering at him. I've known Akin most of my life, and it's clear that he doesn't particularly like Permiton. He certainly doesn't trust him. And how can I blame him? We don't really know Permiton. Nor do we know River and Brook that well. Before all of this, it was me and Akin against the world, but now we both have three others that we must contend with. It's hard for me to imagine trusting these men the way I trust Akin.

And Permiton wants us to just be patient? Patience isn't something I have in abundance at the moment. Especially not when we're this close to Oceana, close to Bright Waters, close to a cure for my mother. Every day we're away from Altinna, she could die. If the poison she drank doesn't kill her, she and my family could be casualties of war if my barrier doesn't hold up.

There are so many "what-ifs," and there isn't time to lose. We have to get to Bright Waters. I can't let Mother down, not when we've already gotten this far.

"What exactly are we waiting for?" Akin asks, his voice low, his eyes narrowed as he looks at Permiton. He's been patient, far more patient than River, but I can hear the edge of frustration creeping in. It's as if he can read my thoughts, and he's in tune with my own frustrations and anxieties.

Permiton finally turns to face us, his expression as blank as ever.

"A way across, of course," he tells Akin with a curt nod.

"And you're sure we won't be noticed?" Brook asks. His voice is soft, almost hesitant, but I can see the flicker of fear in his eyes. Returning to Oceana is hard for him, even harder than it is for River. He's been the shadow his whole life, unnoticed, unwanted. Now, he's public enemy number one, and it's my fault. I can't imagine how difficult it must be to return to a home that no longer claims you.

River steps forward, frustration written all over his face. "You're not going to just tell us what's going on, are you?" he grunts, getting in Permiton's face. "You're going to keep playing these mysterious little mind games while we stand here with nothing but faith in you. And in case you've forgotten, this is now enemy territory for all of us."

River doesn't do quiet despair. His problems become everyone's problems, clearly. He isn't wrong, though. This is enemy territory now, especially for the former princes. Especially for me. Oceana has declared war on Altinna. Permiton is the only one who could reasonably be here without any trouble.

I glance at River, catching his eye, and try to keep my voice calm. "Maybe we should consider another option," I suggest. "What if we wait for a ferry to cross? Surely, someone from Oceana will come over to this side eventually. We could catch a ride back with them."

River just scowls, and Brook shakes his head, rising and coming to stand next to us, a grim look on his face.

"It's not that simple, unfortunately," he tells me quietly. "The narwhals are selective and judicious. They don't take exiles or enemies across the water. They'll try to drown us if we even attempt it."

A chill runs down my spine at Brook's words. Oceana is clearly not a friendly place for its enemies. I can't imagine what it must feel like for River and Brook, knowing they can't return home because they've been rejected by their own family, their own kingdom.

"If the narwhals won't take us, then maybe we pay someone," I suggest, trying to keep my hope alive. "We offer someone on the Oceanean side money, and they can bring us across without asking too many questions. Money talks, right? As you're always reminding us," I shoot at River.

Akin gives me a skeptical look, but before he can respond, Permiton holds up his hand.

"We won't need to resort to that," he tells us, cryptic as ever.

I wish I could see into his mind, to understand what he sees and know what he knows. So far, he's kept all of his plans very close to his chest. It's not that I need to be in charge, but it would help to know something, to have some kind of idea of what will happen next, rather than just standing uselessly on the bank of a large lake, waiting for... something, apparently.

I open my mouth to argue with him, to demand answers, but just then, something moves in the mist ahead. A dark shape glides silently through the water, slowly coming into view. A ferry.

It's beautiful, a sleek and elegant vessel, the wood polished to a high, dark gloss. The mist swirls around it like a cloak, the faint outlines of large, enchanted narwhals visible just beneath the surface of the water as they guide the ferry across. My breath catches at the sight. As it gets closer, I can see a crest on the bow. It's a royal ferry, meant for dignitaries and nobles.

"We might not need to pay after all," I whisper, a small flicker of hope igniting in my chest.

But then, behind the first ferry, more shadows appear. Several ferries, gliding through the mist in a perfect line, like phantoms materializing from the depths of the water.

"Shit," River whispers under his breath, and I hear the sound of Akin unsheathing his sword.

At first, I can't understand their reactions, but then it hits me. The sinking realization, cold and hard, slams into my chest. This isn't just a ferry crossing. It's the Oceanean army. They're coming straight toward us, and if they capture us, we're doomed.

My stomach drops. My hands instinctively curl into fists at my sides, and every muscle in my body tenses, ready to bolt.

"Permiton," I whisper harshly, my voice shaking, "that's the army. We need to hide. Now."

He doesn't move. He doesn't even blink. He stands there, calm and collected, his eyes fixed on the approaching ferries. It's odd and eerie. Off-putting, to say the least. Brook and River stand ready to fight as well, but the five of us can't take on an entire army. We need to run, and it needs to be now. They're coming very quickly.

"What are you doing?" I demand, panic rising in my throat. "We have to get out of sight right now!"

Akin steps forward, his voice a low, urgent growl.

"Permiton, we need to leave. Now. We're not going to win this fight."

But Permiton remains still. "No," he says softly. "We stay."

"Permiton," I hiss. "Please, we have to go."

His cold, blank eyes turn on me, and I can't discern anything that's going through his mind. I want to trust him, to believe in whatever plan he has, but he isn't giving me any reason to. I look at River and Brook, their faces pale and tense, and a wave of fear crashes over me. What is Permiton thinking? The army is almost upon us, and we're standing here like sitting ducks. If they see us, if they recognize River and Brook, we're finished.

"We won't run," Permiton says calmly as he gently grabs my wrists and looks into my eyes. "Trust me."

Trust him? Trust him to get us captured by the very people who want us dead? My mind spins, trying to find another solution, but before I can act, it's too late. The first ferry reaches the shore, and soldiers begin disembarking, clad in Oceanean armor, their weapons gleaming in the dim light.

I take an involuntary step back, my pulse racing. The soldiers are efficient, disciplined, and they move like a well-oiled machine. This isn't a small scouting party. This is an invasion force.

Akin's hand tightens around the hilt of his sword, his eyes locked on the approaching soldiers. He looks ready to fight, but I know we're outnumbered, and there's no way we can win in a direct confrontation. We're trapped.

A tall, imposing man with cold blue eyes, steps forward. Based on his armor, I would guess he's Commander Heela of the Oceanean army. His gaze sweeps over us, lingering on River and Brook for a moment longer than the others. I can see the recognition flicker in his eyes, though he doesn't immediately react.

"Who are you?" he demands, his voice sharp.

I feel my heart hammering in my chest, and I brace myself to run, to fight, anything to get out of this, but Permiton steps forward before I can move.

"We are travelers," Permiton says smoothly, his tone respectful but firm. "From Altinna."

I stare at him, my mouth going dry. What's his endgame? Why would he reveal that?

Heela's eyes narrow. "Travelers from Altinna, you say?"

"Yes," Permiton continues, apparently unfazed. "This is Princess Maerilee of Altinna, and these are her companions. Akin, her bodyguard. River and Brook, exiled princes of Oceana, and I am Permiton, advisor to the queen of Altinna."

My blood runs cold, and my pulse quickens. A pit of dread forms in my stomach. Was this his plan all along?

"And what are you doing here?" Heela asks, his gaze hardening.

Permiton smiles faintly, a glint in his eyes. "My companions have come seeking a miracle, but I know no such miracle exists," he says slowly, his words measured and careful. "I thought that I might garner some favor with the king and queen. I've delivered them to be captured."

For a moment, everything goes silent. The world tilts on its axis, and I feel like I've been punched in the gut. Permiton's words hang in the air, heavy and damning.

He brought us here to be captured?

I stare at him, disbelief and betrayal coursing through me like ice. I don't understand. Why would he do this? Why would he lead us straight into a trap?

The commander smiles, a slow, predatory grin that makes my skin crawl.

"Very well," he says, motioning to his soldiers. "Take them."

3

BETRAYAL

I can't believe it. My heart sinks deep into my chest as Commander Heela approaches, his soldiers swiftly surrounding us, their weapons gleaming in the faint light. I feel the sting of betrayal, sharp and cold, radiating through me like ice. Permiton stands there, so calm, so collected, while we're about to be captured.

"How could you?" I hiss under my breath, barely able to contain the fury bubbling inside me. My hands shake, clenched at my sides. Permiton doesn't even look at me. He moves to stand behind Heela as if he's always belonged there. His expression is infuriatingly calm, like this is all going according to some master plan. But I can't see the plan. All I see is betrayal.

And then everything happens at once.

Before I can even blink, River and Brook surge forward, their hands outstretched. The air around us shivers, the tension crackling like lightning. I feel the pull of their magic immediately, the water in the air responding to their commands. In an instant, the calm surface of the lake behind us erupts, sending crashing waves toward the soldiers, water wrapping around their bodies like living ropes, pulling them down.

"Don't just stand there!" River shouts, his voice sharp with frustration, his eyes burning with intensity. He's not waiting for a plan; he's going to fight his way out of this. Brook, usually so quiet and reserved, is right there with him, his focus laser-sharp as he channels his magic. A spray of water rises from the river and solidifies into sharp, jagged ice spears that he sends flying toward the soldiers.

The soldiers are momentarily stunned by the sudden attack, but they recover quickly, forming a defensive line as they counter the magic with their own. Their weapons glow faintly with enchantments, cutting through the water and ice like it's nothing more than air. It's clear these are seasoned warriors, and they won't go down easily.

Akin, ever the soldier, doesn't hesitate for a second. He charges into the fray, his blade flashing as he slices through the nearest soldier's defenses. His movements are swift and precise, a deadly dance of skill and power. For a moment, I think we might actually have a chance. Between River and Brook's magic and Akin's fighting prowess, we're holding our own.

But there are too many of them. I can see it, feel it in the way the soldiers close in tighter, their formation unwavering despite our best efforts. We're surrounded, and we're outnumbered.

I reach deep inside myself, searching for the magic I know is there, the barrier magic that's slowly weaving together, but it's weak, too weak. Without Permiton's strength, without his connection to me, my barrier is flimsy, like a thin wall of glass that could shatter at any moment.

"Permiton!" I call out, desperation clawing at my throat. "I need your help!"

He doesn't respond. He stands there with his arms clasped behind his back, watching the battle unfold with an infuriating look of indifference, as if none of this matters to him. As if we don't matter to him.

I grit my teeth, pushing harder, trying to force the barrier into place. It flickers around us, shimmering faintly in the air, but it's not enough. The soldiers push through it like it's simply mist.

I scream in frustration, pouring every ounce of strength I have into the magic, but it's no use. I can feel the threads of power unraveling, slipping through my fingers like sand.

Without Permiton's help, without his magic to anchor mine, I can't hold the barrier.

A sharp pain shoots through my chest, not from any physical blow, but from the realization that we're going to lose. Despite everything, we're going to be captured. And Permiton…. I cry out in anguish at his betrayal.

After everything we went through, after he made me trust him, he's turning his back on us like we're nothing. If being with me hadn't strengthened my magic, I might have believed that he planned this from the beginning, that he lied just to gain my trust. But he did strengthen my magic. Our connection is undeniably real.

How could he do this to us? How could he do this to me? I shake my head, the anger a punch to the gut as I keep trying to erect some sort of protective barrier.

I can't let this happen.

But the tide of battle is turning against us. The soldiers press in closer, their enchanted weapons cutting through River and Brook's water magic with brutal efficiency. Akin is a force to be reckoned with, but even he can't take on an entire army by himself. He's slowing, his movements more labored, the weight of the battle taking its toll.

A loud crack splits the air as one of Brook's ice spears shatters against a soldier's shield. Brook staggers back, his face pale, sweat dripping down his brow. River is breathing hard, his jaw clenched in fury, but even he can't keep up the relentless assault forever.

I try to focus, to summon my magic again, but I can't. My body feels drained, my energy sapped. I can barely stand, let alone summon the kind of power I need to protect us.

And then the soldiers are on us.

One grabs me from behind, his arm locking around my throat as he pulls me back. I struggle, kicking out, but he's too strong. Another soldier strikes Akin hard across the chest, sending him sprawling to the ground. I hear him grunt in pain, but he pushes himself up again, refusing to stay down.

"Get off her!" River yells, his voice raw with rage. He throws out his hand, sending a wave of water crashing into the soldier holding me. The force knocks him back, and I stumble forward, gasping for breath.

But it's too late. More soldiers close in around us, their weapons raised, and we have no more room to fight. We're surrounded.

I glance at River, his chest heaving, his eyes wild with frustration. Brook stands beside him, his hands trembling with exhaustion. Akin is on his knees, bleeding from a deep gash across his arm. Meanwhile, Permiton still stands behind the commander, his expression calm, untouched by the chaos around him.

"Permiton!" I scream, my voice breaking with the heavy emotion. "Why are you doing this?"

He meets my gaze, but there's no emotion in his eyes. "Because this is what's necessary," he says quietly, his voice barely audible over the sounds of battle.

I want to fight. I want to scream with rage and tear the world apart, but I can't. My body is spent, my magic drained. We've lost.

The soldiers close in, binding our hands behind our backs with enchanted ropes that burn against my skin. I struggle weakly, but it's no use. We're captured.

I glance at Akin, his face twisted in pain but defiant as ever. He meets my gaze, his eyes filled with silent determination. He hasn't given up, even now. Neither have River and Brook. They're exhausted, beaten, but their spirits haven't been broken. Not yet.

But as the soldiers drag us away, I can't shake the overwhelming sense of betrayal that gnaws at me. Permiton, who I thought was one of us, who I trusted, is the reason we're in this situation. He's the reason we've lost before we even had a chance to truly begin.

And I don't understand why.

As we're marched away from the makeshift battlefield, my mind races, trying to make sense of it all. There has to be a reason, some explanation, for why Permiton did this. But no matter how hard I try to rationalize it, all I can feel is the sharp sting of betrayal.

I trusted him. And he's letting us be led off as prisoners.

The soldiers lead us to a small, makeshift camp at the edge of the forest. They shove us into a cramped tent, binding our hands to the posts inside. They put a pair of cuffs on me that immediately neutralizes all my magic. I feel it the moment they're locked around my wrists. It's like a piece of me is pulled out of my body. It's a strange sensation that leaves me feeling dizzy.

I glance around at the others, each of them tied up. River and Brook both have the same cuffs on, I notice. I guess that they're bound by cuffs that also stop their powers. River's jaw is clenched so tight I can see the muscles twitching, and Brook's eyes are dark with a quiet fury I've yet to experience from him. Akin has an impassive face of calm, as always, though I can see the exhaustion in his posture, the strain of the last hour weighing him down.

His cuffs look the most uncomfortable. I can hear the sizzle of his skin each time his wrists touch the side of the metal. He doesn't complain, doesn't even wince, but I can see the tension in his jaw each time he tries to adjust his hands behind him. It's agony seeing him like this.

None of us speak. The air between us is thick with unspoken words, with anger, confusion, and a sense of defeat that we're all trying to push away.

Eventually, River breaks the silence, his voice low and dangerous. "What the hell is Permiton playing at?"

"I don't know," I admit, my throat tight. "But whatever it is, we need to figure a way out of this. Fast."

Brook shifts uncomfortably, glancing toward the entrance of the tent as if expecting someone to burst in at any moment. "Do you think he's working for them? That he's been playing us this whole time?"

I shake my head, though I'm not entirely sure. "I don't know. It doesn't make sense. Why would he go through all of this with us, help us as much as he did, only to betray us now? He must have a plan. There has to be more to this than we can see right now."

River scoffs in disbelief, rolling his eyes, and Akin just grunts. Brook, per usual, stays quiet in contemplation.

I want to believe him. I want to believe that Permiton has some master plan, that this is all part of some elaborate scheme to protect us. But the betrayal still stings too deeply, and doubt gnaws at the edges of my mind.

The flap of the tent rustles, and we all freeze, our eyes snapping to the entrance. A figure steps inside, and for a brief, fleeting moment, I hope it's Permiton here to explain his plan.

But it's not. It's Commander Heela.

He steps inside, his cold blue eyes sweeping over us with a look of satisfaction. "Comfortable, are we?" he sneers.

River glares at him, his eyes burning with barely contained fury. "What do you want?"

Heela smirks. "I already have what I want. You captured an Altinna on the brink of destruction."

My heart pounds in my chest. "What are you going to do with us?"

He steps closer, his smile widening. "That depends on what your friend Permiton decides."

The mention of Permiton's name sends another wave of confusion and anger through me. What does Heela mean by that? What is Permiton deciding?

He turns to leave, but before he does, he glances over his shoulder, his expression darkening. "I'd get comfortable if I were you. You'll be here for the night ."

And then he's gone, leaving us in the suffocating silence of the tent, the weight of his words hanging heavy in the air.

"What now?" Brook asks, his voice barely above a whisper.

I don't have an answer. All I know is that we can't stay here. We have to get out, somehow, and find out what Permiton is really planning.

But deep down, a cold fear gnaws at me. What if Permiton's betrayal is real? What if we've already lost?

4

PRISONERS

Pale sun filters into the tent, and I blearily open my eyes, for a moment forgetting where I am, how desperate our situation is. Then, the cold iron cuffs bite into my wrists as I sit up, and I remember exactly what's happened. Permiton betrayed us. Akin, River, Brook and I are all prisoners in exchange for... what, exactly? His freedom? Refuge in Oceana while the war wages on?

Whatever Permiton has gotten out of this deal, I can't imagine that it would be worth betraying us. I would never do that to anyone, but definitely not to the person I'm supposed to be mated to for an eternity. Sure, our situation is unusual, but we are bound to each other regardless of what he's done. Those are the ancient laws that come from having a One.

As I turn the situation over and over in my head, the Commander Heela enters the tent. From my place in the dirt, I glare at him with all the hate I can muster. His smirk is infuriating, smug and cruel, as if he's savoring the sight of us, bound and powerless. River and Brook stir beside me, both of them shackled with cuffs infused with fire agate, their water magic rendered completely useless. I can see the frustration burning in their eyes, but they say nothing. Not yet.

"I must say," Heela says as he crouches down to our level, his voice smooth and arrogant, "it's been a long time since I've seen such a valuable group of prisoners."

He walks around us slowly, inspecting us like we're some kind of prize he's won. My stomach churns with anger and fear, but I hold my head high, refusing to give him the satisfaction of seeing how afraid I feel. Even if these cuffs infused with a rare amethyst are sapping my magic completely, I won't let him see me as weak.

"You are especially valuable, Princess," he continues, grabbing my face and forcing me to look him in the eye. His own gleam with malicious satisfaction. "The king and queen sent word about you. You are a freak among fae, and the price on your head is extraordinary. I am very eager to collect."

Akin struggles against his shackles, trying to get to Commander Heela, but he's met with a swift kick in the stomach as the man gets up and circles to River and Brook.

"And as for you two," he sneers darkly, "I'm surprised you thought showing your face here would be a good idea. Neither of you are welcome in this land for the rest of your days. But, since you've stubbornly decided to come on your own, I think the royal dungeons will make an excellent home for you."

River glares at him but says nothing. I can feel the tension radiating off him, his fists clenched so tightly, I'm surprised he hasn't broken skin. Brook sits silent as well, his expression hard and unreadable, though I can see the faint tremor in his hands.

"And of course," he continues, turning his attention to Akin, "your loyal bodyguard. We wouldn't want to forget about him, would we?"

I glance at Akin, my heart aching at the sight of him. He's bound in iron chains, and I can see the pain etched into his face. The chains burn him, searing his skin every time they touch, and yet, he bears it in silence. His jaw is clenched, his eyes narrowed with quiet resolve, but I can see the agony beneath the surface.

I can't stand it. The sight of him like this, suffering in silence, is too much. I stand up, ignoring the sharp pull of the cuffs on my wrists, and glare at Heela. "He's not part of this," I scream, my voice shaking with fury. "Let him go, or at least bind him with something else. Rope. Anything but iron."

Commander Heela raises an eyebrow, clearly amused by my outburst. "You're not in a position to make demands, Princess," he snickers with an arrogant grin.

"I don't care," I snap, my voice rising. "You can't treat him this way. He's done nothing to you."

His smile widens, and he takes a step closer, looking down at me with a patronizing gaze. "Oh, but you see, I'm not taking any chances," he growls lowly. "Your little bodyguard is dangerous, and iron is the only thing that ensures he stays docile."

Docile. The word makes my blood boil. Akin is many things, but he is not docile. He's a warrior, and the idea of him being reduced to this, bound and suffering in silence, makes me want to tear these chains off and fight back. But I can't. Not without my magic.

Permiton enters the tent then, moving to stand off to the side, still unbound and untouched, as if he's not a prisoner at all. The sight of him standing there, completely at ease while we suffer, sends a fresh wave of betrayal through me.

"Permiton," I say, my voice tight with anger. "You can't let this happen. They're going to kill us."

He doesn't answer or even look at me. He just keeps standing there in silence, his expression calm and indifferent. It's as if I don't even exist to him anymore.

I grit my teeth, my hands clenching into fists. I don't understand why he's doing this. Why he's standing there, free and untouched, while the rest of us are treated like prisoners. How could he betray us like this?

"You're going to regret this," I mutter under my breath, though I'm not sure if I'm talking to Permiton or Heela anymore.

He simply chuckles and exits the tent where a group of his soldiers are standing at attention, waiting for his instruction.

"Prepare them for transport," I hear him bark his orders. "We're taking them back to the Oceanean palace."

My stomach clenches at the mention of the palace. I know what that means. We're going straight into the heart of Oceana, into the hands of River and Brook's father, the king who disowned them and declared war on my kingdom. If we make it to the palace, I don't know what will happen to us. But I know it won't be good.

The soldiers move quickly, binding River and Brook's hands behind their backs with more of the fire agate cuffs, ensuring they can't use their water magic. They both resist at first, but the soldiers are quick and efficient, overpowering them with sheer numbers. I can see the frustration in River's eyes as the fire agate saps his strength, rendering him powerless.

Akin is still bound in the iron chains, and I can see the strain on his face as they drag him to his feet. I want to scream, to demand again that they take the chains off, but I know it's useless. Commander Heela isn't going to listen to me.

They don't even let me walk. Instead, they bind me to a horse, my wrists secured to the saddle in front of me, and lead me behind Heela's horse like a prisoner being paraded through the streets. The humiliation stings, but it's nothing compared to the anger boiling inside me at the way they're treating Akin.

The others are forced to march behind the horses, their wrists bound, their heads down. I can hear River muttering under his breath, cursing the commander and the soldiers with every step, but he doesn't have the strength to fight back. Not with his powers sapped.

I look behind to see Akin's face is pale, his steps slow and labored as the iron burns into his skin. Every step he takes sends a fresh wave of pain through him, but he doesn't complain. He doesn't say a word.

I can't stand it.

"You can't treat him this way," I say again, my voice hoarse from shouting. "He's a person, not some animal you can torture!"

Heela ignores me, his eyes focused straight ahead as we parade toward the narwhal-pulled ferry waiting at the edge of the water.

I pull at the cuffs around my wrists, trying to summon even the smallest spark of magic, but the amethyst holds firm, neutralizing every bit of power I try to call forth.

"You're lucky we found those," he shouts back to me, as if he's been watching me struggle with my cuffs. "That's a rare amethyst, and we only found enough to make the one pair. We knew one day we'd encounter a fae with extraordinary power, and we'd need to neutralize their magic. Those cuffs have been waiting for you."

The thought of being completely powerless, of having no control over what happens next, makes my chest tighten with fear. Does this mean my barrier is unable to stand back home? As horrible as this situation is, I can't help but worry about my family, about my mother confined to that room. Without my barrier, they're as good as dead.

Then again, so are we. I can't imagine the king and queen showing us any mercy. They were both so angry when they left my palace. The way they looked at me, at their own sons, it's clear they think I'm some kind of evil, depraved fae. It's not as if I chose this. I'd do anything to just be normal, to have just a single One like everyone else. But that is not the hand I was dealt by the fates, and it isn't my fault.

I'm so lost in my pitiful thoughts, I hardly notice when we begin to slow. As we reach the edge of the water, I see the narwhal-pulled ferry waiting for us, its sleek shape cutting through the mist like a ghostly figure. It's eerily beautiful, the way it glides across the water, the massive narwhals beneath the surface guiding it with quiet grace.

The commander dismounts, turning to his soldiers. "Load them onto the ferry," he demands.

The soldiers move quickly, dragging us toward the ferry. River and Brook are forced to climb aboard first, their hands still bound, their expressions dark and brooding. Akin follows, his steps faltering as the iron chains dig deeper into his skin. I'm led last, still bound to the horse, until they unhook me and shove me forward onto the ferry.

I stumble as I'm pushed aboard. I catch myself on the railing, my wrists still bound tightly in front of me. The ferry sways slightly beneath my feet, the water lapping gently against the sides as the narwhals begin to move.

I glance over at Permiton who stands near Heela, still free, still untouched by all of this. He's chatting with the man as if they're old friends, laughing and smiling like he's not part of the reason we're all here. My stomach twists with anger and confusion. I don't understand what's going on. I don't understand why he's doing this.

As the ferry glides across the water, the mist swirling around us, I feel a deep sense of dread settle over me. We're heading straight into the heart of Oceana, and I have no idea what's waiting for us on the other side. We might be killed straight away, or tortured. The king may decide to keep us as political prisoners for years. There's simply no telling what he plans to do with us.

But one thing is certain: I'm not going to let them win. I'm not going to let them break me. I'll find a way out of this. I have to.

For Akin. For River and Brook. For my family. For my kingdom.

And, just as importantly, for myself.

5

UNEXPECTED VISITORS

The journey on the ferry takes several hours, and they leave us bound on the deck, the bright sun beating down on us. My wrists ache from the tightness of the amethyst cuffs, and my mind feels even more constricted, trapped in a loop of disbelief and betrayal as I watch Permiton making friends with the soldiers.

He's sold us out.

The thought circles over and over in my head, like a vulture picking at the remnants of a dead animal. I keep replaying the last few days in my head, remembering the moment Mother first introduced him to the court, when he cornered me and told me that we would need to connect for my power to fully be realized.

I want to retch as I think of him touching me, of him inside me. Was he planning this even then? Perhaps he was even in on the plot to poison Mother. After all, he's from Ambrosia. Surely, he knew Diereken. They've probably been in on this together, plotting our downfall from the moment they came to Altinna.

I turn my gaze toward him, still sitting near Heela laughing and chatting as if nothing in the world is wrong. His voice carries through

27

the whistling wind, casual and jovial, like this is some kind of holiday, and not a nightmare we've all been dragged into.

My stomach churns with anger, the fire of betrayal burning hotter with every passing moment.

"You're a coward!" I shout, my voice rising, shaking with the fury building inside me. "I trusted you, Permiton. We trusted you! And you betrayed us!"

He ignores me. I see Heela glance my way, but he merely chuckles at Permiton's indifference, as if my anger is some kind of joke.

"You'll pay for this," I say, my voice quieter now, but no less fierce. "You think you've won, but I swear to you, Permiton, I will make sure you regret every moment of this."

Still nothing. Just more laughter, more casual conversation as if nothing has changed between us. It's infuriating.

I grit my teeth and glance over at the others. River, Brook, and Akin are tied to the base of the mast a short distance away. Their wrists are bound tightly, and I can see the faint glow of fire agate on River and Brook's cuffs. But it's Akin who worries me the most. The iron chains they've used to bind him are burning his flesh, and even from here, I can see the raw, blistering wounds on his arms. His face is set in a mask of pain, though he tries to hide it.

I can't stand it. My chest tightens as I watch him suffer, his skin searing beneath the iron, and yet he remains silent, determined not to show weakness.

I won't let him suffer like this. I can't.

I push myself up, wincing as the cuffs dig into my wrists, and march toward the Commander Heela.

"You need to release Akin," I say, my voice firm. "You can't keep him chained like that. It's torturing him."

He looks at me with a raised eyebrow, clearly unimpressed by my demands. "Even if I cared about what you want, he's a dangerous man, Princess," he spits. "I'm not taking any chances."

"Rope," I insist, desperation creeping into my voice. "Bind him with rope. You don't need iron chains."

He smirks, his cold eyes gleaming. "I'll be the one to decide what I'm going to use to keep him under control."

I open my mouth to argue further, but Permiton's voice cuts in before I can say another word. "Leave it, Maerilee," he says smoothly, his eyes still on the commander. "It's not worth the trouble."

I whirl on him, my rage boiling over. "Not worth the trouble?" I roar. "Akin is being burned alive because of those chains, and you're telling me it's not worth the trouble?"

Permiton shrugs, utterly indifferent. "He'll survive," he answers simply.

The sheer coldness of his words leaves me speechless for a moment. I can't believe this is the same man who told me to trust him, who promised to help me save my mother and erect a strong barrier for Altinna.

He fooled all of us, my mother included, and that's what hurts the most. He gave me hope that we might save her, that together we could do anything. It was Permiton who suggested Bright Waters in the first place, but now I see it was all a ruse. He brought us here to get us out of the way, one last loose end to tie up so his buddy, the crown prince of Ambrosia, can destroy my kingdom.

Even in my chains, I wonder how hard it would be to gauge his eyes out.

Heela waves me off with a dismissive gesture. "We're almost to shore, Princess." He waves dismissively. "Your pleading won't change anything."

My fists clench at my sides, but I know it's no use. They won't listen to me. They don't care about Akin's suffering, and they certainly don't care about any sense of decency or honor.

I'm just a prisoner to them, a spoil of war.

With a heavy heart, I return to my spot on the deck, glancing back at Akin as I sit down. His eyes meet mine for a moment, and though he doesn't speak, I can see the pain in his gaze. He's suffering, and there's nothing I can do to stop it. I feel powerless, and that sense of helplessness digs into me as sharply as the amethyst cuffs around my wrists.

The ferry slows as we reach the other side of the massive lake, and the soldiers prepare us to go ashore. They roughly grab my Three, forcing them up despite protests. River is seething, calling some of them by name and telling them how severely he'll punish them when this mess is sorted, and he's their king. Brook tells him to shut up, and I agree that we'd all be better for it.

We're all dragged off the ferry, as if Heela doesn't trust that we'll walk off on our own. It's not as if we have anywhere else to go; the unnecessary roughness is overkill at this point. He just wants us to show us how powerful he is, how merciless he is. He wants to intimidate us, but I refuse to show any weakness. He won't get the satisfaction from me.

I'm lifted back onto the horse as Heela tells us that we have a several-day journey to the castle. Permiton is also offered a horse, given the honor to ride next to the commander rather than behind him. I want to scream my head off at him, to throw every insult I can think of at him, but I know it's better to save my strength.

We ride for hours, at a slow pace since they're forcing River, Brook, and Akin to walk. My heart aches for them, angry at their despicable treatment. Finally, we stop and the soldiers set up camp.

Heela instructs a soldier to get me a thin, scratchy blanket to sleep on. "Don't let it be said I treat women without any respect," he smirks, a wicked glint in his eye.

The soldiers build a massive fire, cooking a hearty dinner that they purposely deny us. We're fed stale bread and dirty water "to help keep up our strength" but nothing more. We're tied up a distance from the fire, so we're literally out in the cold. The thin blanket does basically nothing to protect me from the chill.

As the night wears on, the soldiers settle into their watch. Four of them stand guard over us, their expressions unreadable in the flickering firelight. I shiver as the chill of the new moon night settles over us, the only source of warmth the dwindling fire nearby.

I glance around, my heart heavy with the weight of everything that's happened. The firelight dances across the trees, casting long shadows that flicker and sway in the wind. There's something eerie about the darkness of the new moon, like the world is holding its breath, waiting for something to break the silence. And then I hear a rustling in the bushes nearby.

My pulse quickens. I sit up a little straighter, watching as two of the guards exchange a glance before moving toward the noise, their hands on the hilts of their swords. They grab a torch from the fire, lighting it quickly before stepping into the darkness.

I watch them go, my heart pounding in my chest. For a brief, desperate moment, hope flares in my chest. Could it be help? Could someone have followed us, come to rescue us? I hold my breath, praying, willing it to be true.

Then the fire goes out.

The darkness swallows us whole, the fire snuffed out in an instant, leaving nothing but inky blackness stretching in every direction. My breath catches in my throat, fear prickling at the edges of my mind. The only sound I hear is the rustling of the leaves, the soft creak of leather armor as the guards move in the darkness, their steps growing fainter.

"River?" I whisper, barely audible in the darkness.

"I'm here," he replies, his voice low and tense. "Stay quiet."

I can't see anything, not even the faintest glimmer of light. The world is pitch black around me, and for the first time since this nightmare began, a real sense of fear takes hold of me. There's something wrong, something unnatural about this darkness. It feels thick, oppressive, like it's pressing down on me, suffocating me.

The rustling in the bushes grows louder, closer now, and I feel a chill run down my spine. I can't see what's happening, but I can sense something is out there, something potentially dangerous.

I hear a soldier scream out in pain, the sound of a sword being plunged through him and the man hitting the forest floor. Then there's more noise as the soldiers who'd settled in for the night come out of their tents, looking to see what's happened.

I glance toward the others, my eyes straining in the darkness, but I can't see them. I can't see anything. The fear tightens in my chest, threatening to overwhelm me, but I force it down. I can't lose control. Not now.

"What's happening?" Brook whispers, his voice barely carrying in the darkness.

"I don't know," I reply, trying to keep my voice steady. "But whatever it is, we need to be ready."

"Ready for what?" River mutters, his tone sharp with frustration. "We're bound and powerless."

The truth of his words stings. We're bound, powerless, and completely at the mercy of whatever is out there. And for the first time, I realize just how vulnerable we are.

The air is still, the darkness stifling. My breath comes in shallow gasps as I strain to hear anything, any sign of what's happening. It's chaos around us, but I can't make out what's actually happening beyond the sounds of fighting. Someone is attacking the Oceanean army, that's for sure, but there's no telling if they're friend or foe.

And then, without warning, a figure emerges from the darkness.

I can't see their face, but they are large, imposing. I can barely make out the shadow of a large sword, and I gasp, terrified of what is going to happen next. I squeeze my eyes shut, bracing myself for the possibility that this might be one of my last moments on this earth.

Then I pass out.

6

THE REBELS

The world comes back to me in bits and pieces. Blurred shadows shift above, and damp earth presses into my back, grounding me as I try to gather my senses. I blink, my vision sharpening gradually, until I see the dense canopy overhead. Water droplets hang from leaves, refracting the faint morning light into tiny rainbows that sway and shimmer as though they're part of a dream. It's quiet here, with only the soft trickle of water nearby and the gentle rustling of wind in the trees. I push myself up on an elbow, and that's when I spot them.

River, Brook, and Akin are huddled around a low fire, surrounded by a group of strangers. My heart leaps as I focus on Akin, his wrists still covered, but not with chains. They're covered in bandages, dark with some sort of balm underneath. His face is pale, but he smiles in the firelight, laughing at something one of the strangers said. Relief floods through me, so overwhelming I nearly sway from it. He's alive. We're all alive.

As if sensing my movement, River looks up, his usual cool gaze softened with something close to concern.

"Maerilee," he says loud enough for me to hear him, nodding to the others. They turn, their faces brightening with cautious relief. Akin is

33

the first to get up, rushing to my side to help me stand. I brush leaves off my clothes and out of my hair as we walk over to the fire together.

The strangers sitting there all watch me curiously, yet somehow, there's a warmth in their eyes, a shared understanding that tells me these people are not like the soldiers we've been running from. A faint glimmer of hope begins to spark within me, tentative but present.

Before I can gather my thoughts, a tall figure stands from the circle, his eyes sharp and assessing but kind. He walks toward me with a grace that speaks of both power and purpose, the kind that only comes from years of command. His cloak shifts in the early morning light, revealing dark green markings of trees and rivers, an homage to the lands we're hiding within.

He halts a few steps away, and to my surprise, bows deeply.

"Princess Maerilee," he says, his voice a low, steady rumble. "I am Caelan Stormrider, a spy for Altinna and the leader of a resistance force here in Oceana."

I blink, struggling to process his words. The flicker of hope turns into a flame as I realize that we have allies now. An entire band of fighters to help us on our quest.

"A spy for Altinna?" I echo, barely able to keep the excitement from my voice. "That's very handy."

"Yes," he replies, his gaze steady. "I've been here for years, building a resistance against the royal family, preparing for the day when Oceana might move against Altinna. I knew it would only be a matter of time."

Out of the corner of my eye, I see River and Brook shift uncomfortably, but Caelan doesn't notice. He continues his story.

"I've watched and waited all this time, hoping it would never come to this, but ready to fight if it did. The news of the invasion reached me days ago, and now that you and your party are here…. " He pauses, his eyes reflecting an intensity I haven't seen in anyone since we began this journey. "Well, I knew I needed to help."

The hope in his voice is genuine, but the bitterness of Permiton's betrayal lingers, tainting my ability to fully trust this stranger. Things didn't end so well the last time I did. I glance at my companions. River looks skeptical, as usual, and Brook's face is guarded, while Akin seems caught between gratitude and physical pain. My heart aches for him.

"So, you've been spying for us all this time?" I ask, needing to hear more, to see if I can find a hole in his tale.

Caelan nods. "It's a long story, but yes, my loyalty lies with Altinna and with Queen Kimalissa. You can choose to believe me or not but know that I've pledged my life to our shared cause. When I heard news of your mother's condition, I knew time was running out. Even if you don't trust me, I pledge my allegiance to you here and now, as the ambassador in your mother's stead."

The sincerity in his voice doesn't waver, yet doubt clings to me from the shadows of my mind. Permiton also pledged his allegiance and vowed to serve my mother, to protect us from our enemies. He said all the right things, only to betray us when we needed him most. And now, here's another man claiming loyalty to Altinna, just when we're at our most vulnerable. It's a miracle—or a con—but I genuinely can't determine which.

"You have a right to your hesitation, Princess," Caelan says, reading my expression with unnerving ease. "But I think you'll find I have no hidden motives here. Our enemy is the same, and I have much to offer in your fight."

He gestures toward the fire where his men are sitting. It isn't a large group, compared to the Oceanean army, but they've proven their strength. They rescued all of us, after all, and they've clearly cared for Akin's wounds.

I cross my arms, considering.

"Trust is earned, of course, and I intend to do just that," Caelan continues, meeting my gaze without faltering. "But if you doubt me now, let me offer you something tangible."

He gestures to one of the rebels beside him, a tall woman with braids in her hair like the roots of an ancient tree. She steps forward, carrying a leather-bound map, frayed at the edges and marked with faint lines in faded ink. Caelan unfolds it, and I realize it's a detailed map of Oceana marked with paths, waterways, and routes that are clearly intended to avoid the usual military outposts.

"We can guide you to our camp where you'll be safe. Our people will care for you until you can get to fighting strength once again." Caelan says, his voice steady. "We've mapped the terrain extensively. My people and I know how to travel through Oceana without drawing attention."

I swallow, unable to ignore the allure of his offer. The map show the entire kingdom with extensive routes through the mountains. Perhaps it can even help lead us to Bright Waters. Without Permiton on our side, we don't have much to go on. If Caelan and his people truly know how to navigate the terrain, this could be the chance we've been hoping for.

I glance at Akin, who gives a small nod, his face still pale but resolute. River and Brook, too, seem to sense the weight of Caelan's offer. The flames flicker across their faces, and their distrust is evident. But so is their resolve. We seem to all understand that these rebels are our best shot of getting to Bright Waters.

"All right, Caelan," I say finally, trying to sound confident. "We'll accept your help. But understand this: if you betray us, if you're leading us into a trap, I will see to it that you regret it."

Magic shoots through my veins, causing a spark at my palms. I can't do much without Permiton here, but it's enough to show I'm serious. It's a party trick at best, but he doesn't need to know that. A faint smile tugs at the corners of his mouth.

"Completely understood, Princess. But you have my word. I will help you get to safety, and when the time comes, I will stand with you against the Oceanean army to fight."

As he goes to sit back down, my gaze drifts to Akin. Up close, I can see how soft and carefully applied the bandages are, and the balm gives off a faint smell of peppermint. He catches my eye and gives a small, reassuring nod, though I can see the exhaustion in his eyes. It's a reminder of everything we've endured to get this far, and I resolve not to let my fears undermine the trust he seems willing to place in

Caelan. Akin has good judgment, I know that. After all, he's not yet come around on River, nor have I.

The rebels settle back down to eat, and I join my friends around the fire, noticing the plates of food they've been given. It's a simple fare of roasted root vegetables and dried herbs but more than we've eaten in days. River hands me a plate, his face unreadable, though he watches Caelan out of the corner of his eye, suspicion lingering in his gaze.

"I don't like him," River mutters under his breath as I sit beside him, picking at the food. "There's something too smooth about him."

I can't help but smirk, thinking that River's distrust is even more reason to trust Caelan. His instincts have been famously wrong so far.

"Says the king of charm," I snip. "You just don't like him because there's someone even smoother than you are."

"Well, at least you admit I'm smooth," he quips back with an eye roll.

Brook looks up from his plate, his gaze shifting between us and Caelan, who's talking quietly with another rebel.

"He has no reason to lie," he says softly. "If he was loyal to Oceana, he wouldn't have rescued us. And he believed our story. He could have put River and I in chains for being Oceanean royalty -"

"Former royalty," River spits, cutting him off.

"But he's treated us with civility and kindness," Brook continues, as if River didn't speak at all.

River huffs but doesn't respond, and we fall into a quiet rhythm of eating, each of us lost in our own thoughts. The weight of our journey so far settles over me, and I'm reminded once more of the responsibility I carry. I don't just have to reach Bright Waters, I also have to return to Altinna with the power to save my mother and re-erect the barrier. There's so much at stake.

Once we finish eating, Caelan motions for us to join him near the water's edge. The forest is dense here, the trees thick with moss and leaves, creating a canopy that hides us from view. It's a strange blend of wilderness and safety, a natural fortress that feels both comforting and ominous.

"Tonight, we'll take you further into the forest, away from any patrol routes," Caelan explains, spreading the map on a smooth rock. He traces a path through the mountains, indicating a hidden route that's far from the main roads.

"The path to our camp is long and treacherous," he warns, glancing between us. "It requires strength and resilience, but with the right guidance, it can be done. If we move swiftly and avoid detection, we should reach it within a day or two."

"Two days," Akin murmurs, his voice low. "And you think we'll make it that far without being caught?"

Caelan's expression remains steady. "With my people, yes. We know these forests better than anyone. But I need you all to trust me and follow our lead."

I study Caelan's face, looking for any hint of deception, but his gaze is calm and open. It's hard not to believe him, hard not to be swept up by the quiet confidence in his words. I know better than to trust so quickly, yet something about Caelan's presence feels genuine, somehow.

"And when we reach your camp?" I ask, my voice barely above a whisper. "What then?"

Caelan grins widely, mirth in his eyes.

"Well, now that you're here, Princess, we have more intel than we've ever had before. We'll be able to plan a major assault on the Oceaneans, cutting them off at the knees before they can even leave for Altinna. "

His words linger heavily in the air, and I can't help but worry. I think of my Four, Akin, River, Brook, and even Permiton, wherever he may be. They are my strength, my source of magic, the force that binds me. Without Permiton, though, my power is weaker, and I don't know how much help I can actually be in the fight. And what about mother? At some point, we'll have to tell Caelan that we need to break off to find Bright Waters. Will he still help us then?

"Thank you, Caelan," I say finally, my voice carrying both gratitude and caution. "We'll follow your guidance, but I want to be clear. You'll answer to me if anything goes wrong."

He inclines his head, bowing slightly at the hips.

"Understood, Princess Marilee. I wouldn't have it any other way."

As the sun rises fully above the trees, casting a bright glow on the forest floor between leaves, I feel a strange sense of peace. For the first time since we set out, there's a plan, a glimmer of hope, and a path forward. We'd be fools not to take it.

7

IT'S A MYTH

Akin

The moment Caelan strode into the Oceanean camp to save us, I recognized his fighting style. There was a rhythm in the way he moved, in the stance he took. It was unmistakably Altinnian, the subtle weight shift, the way his fingers hovered near the hilt of his weapon, always prepared for the unexpected. It was something only someone trained for combat in Altinna would know, and I knew that we were saved. His rescue mission was, obviously, a complete success.

I watch as he talks to Maerilee now, offering her words of assurance with a calm that doesn't waver. When he turns to me, I can't help the grin that pulls at my mouth.

"I'm glad to be fighting alongside another Altinnian," I say, clapping him on the shoulder. "Not to speak ill of Maerilee's other three men, but one was a traitor, and the other two are completely spoiled princes. Literally."

He chuckles, giving a quick nod of acknowledgment. "The training runs deep. I suppose that's a good thing. Oceanean's trust only in their water magic. Their hand-to-hand combat is lacking, to put it mildly."

We settle in by the fire, the others scattered around, resting as best they can after the night's ordeals. The plan is for us to rest for a few hours before we set off for the camp. Caelan says it's much safer to travel by night.

While the others settle in to sleep, I fill Caelan in on everything that's happened in Altinna since the barrier started to weaken, from Queen Kimalissa's failing health to Direken's threats of invasion. The words spill out of me like water from a dam. I'm finally feeling free enough to unburden myself with a fellow soldier.

Caelan listens intently, his expression remaining steady. But when I mention the Bright Waters and our need to reach them, he laughs, his shoulders shaking with genuine amusement. "Bright Waters?" he repeats, his eyes glinting with a trace of disbelief. "You're serious?"

I nod, frowning at his reaction. "Of course I am," I tell him, suddenly feeling slighted. "They're our only chance to save the queen. They hold the power we need to save Queen Kimalissa from the poison she's been given."

Caelan's expression softens, though a trace of humor still lingers in his gaze. "I don't know how to tell you this, Akin, so I'm just going to say it," he says before taking a deep breath. "Bright Waters is a myth. It's just a story used to lure greedy foreigners into the heart of Oceana where they're met with swift justice from the Oceaneans. It's not a place any living soul has ever reached because it doesn't exist."

I go still, Caelan's words slicing through me with a cold, unfamiliar fear. Bright Waters can't be a myth. It is our one hope, the only thing that can save Queen Kimalissa, save Altinna.

I can barely voice the question pressing against my throat. "Are you certain?"

He nods, regret flickering across his face. "I've lived here long enough to hear the legends for what they are. Who was it who told you to go to Bright Waters?"

A chill spreads through me at his question. In all this time, I haven't stopped to wonder or question the validity of this mission. But as I remember how the events unfolded, I remember exactly who it was who started us on this journey.

Permiton.

Of course, it was Permiton who sent us on this journey, Permiton who gave us hope with the promise of a miracle. How convenient, then, that the Oceanean army was ready to meet us so swiftly after we arrived. I can't believe I was so stupid, so trusting. I believed in him for Maerilee's benefit, for Queen Kimalissa's too, but now I realize that it was all a ruse.

Bright Waters doesn't exist. It never did. He never even thought it did. He just wanted to lead us to our deaths.

The fire crackles between us, its warmth unable to cut through the chill settling in my gut. If Bright Waters is nothing but a legend, then what? Everything we've endured, the miles we've crossed, the risks we've taken are all for nothing. We almost died for nothing.

But Caelan's hand claps my shoulder firmly, pulling me from the bleak spiral of my thoughts. "Don't be so glum, my friend," he says, his voice uplifting. "We'll find a way to save the queen. If there's one thing I know about Altinnian fighters, it's that they don't give up when the odds look impossible. You have my support, whatever you need. But I don't want you running after something that doesn't exist."

I nod, but the unease gnaws at me, sinking its claws deep. "I know," I say, though the words feel hollow. "But it's hard to know what to believe now."

Caelan squeezes my shoulder. "Then trust in what you know. Trust your instincts and the strength of those around you."

The truth of his words strikes deep. I've always been a man of instincts, trained to trust my own judgment and make decisions without doubt. But now, when every move feels clouded by uncertainty, even that instinct feels tainted by doubt.

As if summoned by my thoughts, I see Maerilee making her way over, her face shadowed with worry. I give Caelan a nod, letting him know I'll be fine, then turn my attention to her, attempting to meet her gaze with a smile I don't entirely feel.

"Is everything okay?" she asks quietly as she sits down next to me, looping both of her arms through one of mine. "It looked like you were having a pretty intense conversation."

"Everything is fine, love, nothing to worry about," I lie.

She frowns, looking up at me to catch my gaze. "Akin, don't try to play the stoic soldier with me. I know you better than that." Her fingers brush over the edges of the bindings, her eyes narrowing as she inspects the raw skin underneath. "Did they hurt you badly?"

Her voice is small, and her words are laced with emotion. I grab her hand and bring it to my lips to kiss it. I've never had someone care about me like this before. In the army, we're taught to hide our pain, or better yet, not to feel any at all. For years, I've stood by Maerilee's side, silently protecting her and watching out for her safety. It never even occurred to me that one day she might care about mine. The least I can do is trust her the way she's trusted me all these years.

I exhale, letting down the barrier I've kept between us. "My injuries hardly bother me at all," I tell her earnestly. "I've had worse. It's just the uncertainty of everything. I don't even know if we're heading toward something real anymore."

Her eyes soften, and she snuggled herself into my side, close enough that I can feel the warmth radiating from her. "Akin, you don't have to carry this alone. I'm afraid too. I'm angry. I feel betrayed."

Her voice wavers, a flash of vulnerability slipping through the cracks in her armor. And in that moment, I see her not as the princess I've sworn to protect, but as a woman grappling with the same fears, the same doubts, that gnaw at me.

"It was Permiton who sent us after the Bright Waters," she continues, her voice heavy with bitterness. "He gave us hope, but now I have to question everything. He sold us out to those soldiers so easily, he clearly never intended for us to reach Bright Waters. Maybe he poisoned my mother. I just don't know."

I place a hand on her shoulder, grounding her with the only certainty I can offer. "Permiton betrayed us, but that isn't going to stop us from saving the queen. I can promise you that."

She looks up at me, her silver eyes catching the faint glow of the firelight, and for a heartbeat, the burdens we carry seem lighter.

"Thank you, Akin," she whispers, her voice barely audible over the crackle of the fire. "I don't know what I'd do without you."

I want to tell her that I'll always be there for her, that nothing will ever take me from her side. But the words catch in my throat, held back by the knowledge that I'm just one of her Four–a protector, a part of her destiny, but not her only.

Instead, I gently kiss her forehead. "We'll make it through this. All of us."

She nods, though a shadow of doubt still lingers in her eyes. As she rests her head against my shoulder, a surge of determination flares within me. No matter the path we're on, whether we're chasing a myth or something real, I know that my purpose is clear. I have to see Maerilee safely to the end of this journey.

"We should get some rest," I murmur, feeling how heavy her head is against my shoulder. "Would you like to stay in my tent?"

She looks up at me, a lustful gleam in her eye. "Very much so," she whispers.

I hold her hand and guide her to the tent that's been assigned to me. Caelan was thoughtful enough to space the tents far enough away from each other so that we shouldn't be overheard. Hopefully.

When we're safely inside, I pull her down onto the soft bed of grass, and kiss her soundly, the way I've wanted to for days. Unfortunately, we've been surrounded by the prying eyes of her other Three, but now it's just us. I wish it was always just us.

She gasps as my hand slips up the hem of her skirts, caressing the soft flesh of her thigh. Her hands cup my face, and I feel her nod quickly against me as we continue to kiss, our tongues battling for dominance.

She sighs as I slip one finger inside of her warm folds, then another. "Akin," she moans quietly. "More."

I pull away briefly, just to undo my trousers and position myself on top of her. Her head is thrown back, her eyes closed, as she waits for me, but I want to see her. I want to look deeply into her silver pools of desire when I enter her.

"Look at me, Maerilee," I command, something I would never normally do to her.

Her eyes snap open, but rather than arguing, she looks into my eyes, her hands encircling my wrists to pull me back down to her. I prop my weight on my elbow and position myself at her entrance, relishing in the way her eyes widen and her mouth drops open as I slip inside of her.

"More," she demands again, her hips lifting up to meet mine.

I slam into her, as her hips thrash, and we manage to find a hectic rhythm as we lavish each other with deep, frenetic kisses. My hands roam her body, both over and under her dress as hers scrape across my back, scratching hard when I do something that feels particularly good to her.

I try to repeat those movements, or at least mentally save them so I can do them again later, but my mind is hazy with desire. I feel my release nearing, and I want to make sure she's falling over with me.

One of my hands dips down to her warmth, my thumb brushing over her slit until I find the point that makes her nearly scream out. She immediately claps her hand over her mouth, and neither of us can help but to laugh, hoping none of our companions heard that. Then again, I don't think either of us could give a damn if they did.

As waves of pleasure start to roll over me, I move faster inside of her, both with my manhood and my finger, and soon, I can feel her body almost vibrating around me. She's nearly biting her hand now as I feel her body suddenly tense, her walls tightening around me, and then she lets go, her breath coming out in wild spurts as she tries desperately not to make a sound. It's all I need to follow her, breathing a similarly erratic rhythm, our breath creating a strange, primal music that only we can hear.

8

BREEDING MISTRUST

As night begins to fall, we're given the signal to leave our makeshift camp and start our journey to the rebel base. I don't like it. We should be heading to Bright Waters, but of course, no one would listen to me. I'm just the spoiled former crown prince, the one everyone wishes were gone. They'd probably trade me with Permiton in a heartbeat, and that's just if I were lucky. I could have betrayed them, too. At least their disgust with me would be more warranted.

We travel for hours, picking through the harsh terrain by moonlight and dim lanterns. I have to admit, this is part of my country I've never experienced before, and I'd certainly prefer to be doing it in a carriage. I miss the luxuries of my station. Why did I have to give it all up for Maerilee, especially when she doesn't even like me? Not that I like her much. She thought Permiton was one of her Four, so her judgment is clearly not worth anything.

I manage to keep most of my complaints along the way to myself, knowing that I'm outnumbered now more than ever. These people, these low lives, are rebel forces. They'd probably happily take me out and make it look like an accident. If it weren't for Akin telling Caelan all of our secrets, Brook and I probably would be dead, or at the very least in chains. That's one small miracle, I suppose.

But I don't trust Caelan. Maerilee can take stock in that or not, but my instinct tells me that he's leading us astray. We don't need one more traitor in our midst, and he smells of false allegiance. Maerilee and Akin only trust him because he's one of them. My people certainly weren't our allies, why would theirs be?

My rage at the injustices of it all fuels me on until we finally, blessedly, stop just before dawn. Caelan has, apparently, found one of their well-used camping sites. There's even a pit ready for the fire. Thank the gods, I'm absolutely famished. As some of the rebels get the fire going, and Caelan and Akin begin assembling the tents, I collapse on the ground, dreaming of my mattress in the palace. This is a far cry from it.

When I open my eyes, everyone else has gathered around me, and food is being passed around. Brook nudges me to sit up. He's the only person here who actually cares about me.

The firelight flickers across the faces around me, casting sharp shadows over Akin's hardened gaze and Brook's quiet, brooding expression. Caelan is talking again, leaning forward with that calm, calculating look, and I watch him with every ounce of suspicion I can muster. Every word out of his mouth feels like another pebble in the growing pile of mistrust that's lodged itself firmly in my gut. Maerilee sits across from him, her face open and earnest, and I can practically feel the hope bleeding from her with every lie he spins. It's almost painful to watch.

"I was speaking with Akin earlier, and I think there's something you all should know," Caelan says, his gaze sweeping over us with that well-practiced charm. "The Bright Waters are, well, they're a myth. An old story. Something to lure outsiders deep into the mountains where only death awaits. It's an Oceanean tale told to keep people out."

I can tell he's trying to sound gentle, even sincere, but I see right through him. I've heard this story before, but not in the way he's spinning it now. Bright Waters isn't a legend meant to ward people off; it's something we've held close to our hearts in Oceana, a source of magic that only a select few have ever touched or even seen.

But as I look around, I realize I'm the only one in the group who knows this, with the possible exception of my brother. It's always hard to tell from his blank expression. And now, Caelan's standing there, spreading lies with that irritating smirk, and they're all buying it. Even Maerilee, who I thought would be wise enough to see through it, just nods, her expression falling like he's taken away her last hope. My teeth clench at the way her shoulders slump, her gaze drifting down to the ground as though she's struggling to hold on to whatever optimism she has left.

And of course, as if on cue, there's Akin. He's quick to reach out, his hand coming to rest on Maerilee's shoulder in a way that's too familiar, too comforting. I almost snort at the sight. I want to yell out, to tell her that Caelan's feeding them all a carefully crafted lie, but the warmth of Akin's hand on her shoulder, and the soft look she gives him, is a wall I can't breach right now. So I say nothing. Let Akin play the hero. I'm not in the mood to play nice.

After we eat, I lie awake near the fire, staring up at the canopy of branches overhead, feeling the weight of my anger and frustration press down on me like the rough earth beneath my back. I can't believe Caelan. I can't believe Maerilee is trusting him so easily after all we've been through. Doesn't she see it? Doesn't she feel the doubt worming its way in, the same way every instinct in me is screaming that he's lying? I finally fall asleep, feeling deeply disgruntled, but what else is new?

As evening falls once more, we set off toward the mountains, toward Caelan's so-called base camp. We're supposed to be heading for some rebel sanctuary, a safe haven, but the irony doesn't escape me. I grew up in this kingdom. I know the mountains, and I know where the Bright Waters are supposed to be, somewhere deep within those craggy peaks, hidden from anyone who doesn't know what they're looking for. And now here we are, heading right toward them, and no one seems to realize it but me.

Caelan leads us deeper into the heart of Oceana, far beyond the borders where most people live. His rebel camp is hidden in these mountains, supposedly built to shelter his people from the king's wrath. It's smart, I'll give him that. The mountains are nearly impassable, with winding trails and sudden cliffs, but for those who know the paths, they're a fortress. The Bright Waters, if they're real, and I know they are, are just as unreachable for anyone who doesn't know how to find them.

For all I know, Caelan has taken control of them and is blocking our path, trying to distract us from the truth. To what end, I'm not sure, but I'm going to get to the bottom of it.

We continue walking in silence, the air thick with tension, though maybe it's just my own. Every step deeper into the mountains twists the frustration in my chest tighter until I can't tell if I'm furious at Caelan for lying, at Maerilee for believing him, or at myself for not doing more to stop this charade.

And then, finally, I find myself alone with her. Maerilee, her silver hair catching the moonlight in a way that almost makes me forget how angry I am, has broken off from the group who's busy setting up our camp. She stands a few paces away, looking out over the mountainside. I approach her, feeling the weight of everything I've been holding back pressing against my chest.

"You realize he's lying, right?" I say, my voice low but edged with the frustration I can't keep hidden. "Caelan. He's not telling you the truth."

She turns to me, her expression guarded, and I can see the hurt flash in her eyes. "Don't do this, River," she warns. "He rescued us, he's fed us, and he's keeping us safe. How could you accuse him of lying to us?"

"Because I know what I'm talking about," I snap, sharper than I intended. "Bright Waters isn't just some legend to scare off foreigners. It's real. My parents told me about it, told me about the power it holds. And I know how to find it."

She crosses her arms, her expression hardening. "And what if it's just a fairy tale? Something your parents told you as a child? You were the son of the king, for goodness' sake. They probably wanted you to think your land is worth more than it is. It wouldn't surprise me, considering how big your ego is."

I scoff, a bitter laugh slipping out before I can stop it. "You think I don't know the difference between a fairy tale and the truth, Maerilee?" I sneer. "This is my home, these are my mountains. I know what lies out there, and I know Caelan's lying to you."

Her eyes narrow, and for a moment, I see a flicker of the steel that makes her so damn frustrating. "Or maybe," she says slowly, her voice laced with a challenge, "you're just letting your pride get in the way. You don't like him because he's helping us, because he's giving us a chance. You're so suspicious of everyone, River, even when they're trying to help."

I step closer, refusing to back down, even though her words sting more than I'd like to admit. "And maybe you're being naïve," I say, each word measured and cutting. "Putting your trust in all the wrong people because you're so desperate for someone to believe in."

The words hang heavy between us, each accusation slicing deeper than I intended. Her eyes flash, and for a moment, I wonder if she's going to slap me. But instead, she steps forward, closing the gap between us, her voice barely above a whisper but sharp enough to cut. "You don't get to decide who I trust, River," she seethes. "I've had enough people trying to control me, trying to tell me who to believe, who to rely on. I don't need another."

"Is that what you think this is?" I ask, my voice rough with anger. "You think I'm trying to control you? I'm trying to protect you, Maerilee. Because I care."

The words slip out before I can stop them, raw and unguarded, and for a moment, we just stare at each other, the anger and confusion swirling between us like a storm. And then, without thinking, without any intention, my hand reaches out, finding her arm, and I pull her closer.

Our lips meet, harsh and unyielding, fueled by the frustration and tension that never seems to dissipate between us. There's nothing soft about the kiss, nothing gentle. It's a clash of wills, a battle of anger and desire that neither of us is willing to back down from. I feel her hands gripping my arms, her nails digging in as though she's trying to ground herself, and I don't let go, caught in the heat of the moment, in the reckless need to prove something I can't even name.

But then, just as quickly, the reality of it hits, cold and unyielding. I pull back, breathing hard, my heart hammering against my ribs as I look at her, seeing the shock and confusion mirrored in her eyes.

"What was that?" she whispers, her voice barely audible.

I shake my head, the disgust I feel at myself mixing with the anger that still lingers. "A mistake," I spit.

She lets out a shaky breath, her hands dropping from my arms, and I can see the walls going back up, the distance settling between us once more. "Agreed," she says, her voice cold, controlled. "Let's not make it again."

For a moment, we just stand there, the weight of everything unsaid pressing down on us, and I realize that whatever fragile bond we had, whatever trust or understanding we'd been building, has shattered. I've pushed her further away, and now I'm left with nothing but the bitter taste of regret.

Without another word, she turns and walks away, her shoulders rigid, her steps measured. And I'm left standing there, alone on the mountainside, feeling the cold bite of the wind against my skin and wondering just how much damage I've done.

9

———————

THE SPARE

It's been a long two days since our rescue, and tensions are clearly running high. Maerilee and River slipped away to have some kind of argument, and when they came back, they sat on opposite ends of the fire. Maerilee went to sit by Akin, of course, making herself small against him as he wrapped her in his arms.

I feel uncomfortable watching them, but they aren't exactly quiet about their affection for each other. Literally. I could barely sleep the other night, hearing how wild they were for one another. It's unfair to feel jealous about it. I know she didn't choose this life. She wouldn't have chosen all four of us if she'd had any say in the matter.

She loves Akin. She hates River. She... doesn't much seem to notice that I'm around. Not than anyone else does. None of the rebels have spoken to me; they've only spoken around me. River's, surprisingly, been my only real companion on this journey, but only when the mood suits him. Per usual, the mood rarely does, and he often prefers to be on his own, sullen in his misery, or loudly complaining for the whole group to hear. At least, in mixed company, he's stopped being so vocal with his displeasure.

"I thought we would be there by now," I finally voice, my throat hoarse from disuse.

Caelan looks up at me, curiously, a jaunty smile on his face. "He speaks," he muses, his eyes dancing with delight.

"He does," I deadpan. "And he thought you said the camp was only a day or two away. It's been two days. Shouldn't we be there by now?"

"I do apologize, Your Royal Highness," he smirks. "Normally, it takes two days for my soldiers, but you all are unused to such a journey. We're moving a little slower than we normally would."

I look over to see Maerilee blushing and looking humbled. It makes my blood boil, and I immediately regret saying anything. Though Caelan is Altinnian, I don't think he's trying to wound my pride. We probably are genuinely slowing him down. However, we are also nearing Bright Waters, and if we follow him to his camp, we're going to be going in the wrong direction.

I don't care what he's told us. I know that it's real. I've read the ancient texts and the few accounts that exist about the journey. Caelan may believe they're a myth, but that means someone did their job. As an Altinnian, he should believe they're a myth. Bright Waters was given to Oceana as a gift from the gods.

There's no use in arguing, though, not now. Caelan would only publicly call me out.

After we eat, we decide to push a little further, rather than camp down for the day. As we continue up the mountain, the path is narrow, winding around jagged rocks that jut out like the teeth of a sleeping giant. The rest of the group walks ahead, led by Caelan, who seems so sure of where he's taking us. Every time he turns a corner, he strides forward with that irritating confidence, like he knows every inch of this treacherous land. And maybe he does, but something about his unerring direction rubs me the wrong way. He knows the deepest secrets of these mountains, yet he still believes Bright Waters is a myth. He's an ignorant fool.

I follow behind, but my mind isn't here. It's fixed on the waters, on the stories I heard growing up, the quiet whispers of power that ran through our family's lineage like a pulse. And now, as I drag my feet along this miserable mountain trail, the desire to strike out alone and find it myself stirs something deep within me. What if I do? What if I could prove my worth by bringing Maerilee to the Bright Waters alone?

The others won't listen to me, I know that much. Even Maerilee. She's so angry with River, maybe more furious than I've ever seen her, and Akin's the only one she trusts. And because Akin trusts Caelan, she does, too. I try to convince myself it doesn't matter, that I shouldn't feel slighted, but the feeling lingers, gnawing at me like a dull ache I can't shake.

I lag further behind as the group continues around another bend, half-hidden by the mountainside, and something snaps within me. Maybe they don't need me after all. Maybe I don't need them, either.

The idea grows roots. What if I just went after the Bright Waters myself? Maerilee would notice then. She'd have to. Maybe she'd finally see that I could be the one to make a difference, that I have more to offer than just being the quiet, overlooked younger brother.

My heart pounds as I drift further back until I'm nearly out of sight of the others. The thought solidifies, and with a determined exhale, I start gathering my things. I reach for my satchel, wrapping my fingers around the worn leather strap as I consider what I'll need to survive on my own. This isn't like me, and I know it, but there's a surge of something almost reckless in the idea, something that makes me feel like I could finally prove my worth.

Lost in my thoughts, I don't hear the soft steps approaching until they're right behind me. I turn sharply, half-expecting it to be Caelan coming to drag me back with that infuriating smirk. But it's Maerilee. She's standing there, her arms crossed, her expression a mix of curiosity and concern.

"Brook, what are you doing?" Her voice is soft, but there's a hint of steel behind it, the kind that makes me freeze mid-motion, guilt flashing through me.

I clear my throat, struggling to find the right words.

"I was just thinking of heading out," I stutter. "Of finding Bright Waters myself."

She blinks, surprise flickering in her eyes. "Caelan says Bright Waters is a myth," she answers, her voice set with a quiet determination. "And it isn't safe out here alone."

I hesitate, letting out a heavy sigh. She doesn't understand, and I don't know if I can make her see it, but I try anyway. "I just...." I struggle. "I don't know where I fit in this, Maerilee. Everyone has a role, everyone's needed. But me? I don't feel like I belong here. No one would even notice if I disappeared, least of all you. And you may have given up on Bright Waters, but I haven't."

Her expression softens, and she steps closer, her hand resting gently on my arm. "Brook, that's not true. You belong here. With us. With me."

She doesn't argue about Bright Waters, and I can't help but wonder if that's a diplomatic tactic. She thinks I'm crazy, I'm misguided, so she addresses what she knows is true. Even I learned how to do that for my royal duties.

I want to believe her, I really do, but the doubt is like a weight pressing down on my chest. Here, on the side of a mountain, I've finally found the guts to make a stand for myself, to do something unexpected. And even though it means leaving the woman I've given everything up for, I have to be a little proud that I've made such a bold decision.

"But it is true," I say quietly. "You have Akin, and he's always there, always protecting you. And River. Well, he might be an arrogant ass, but he's strong. I don't bring anything to the table. I'm the spare, the tagalong. I'm not a warrior, I'm not—" I trail off, shaking my head. "You don't need me here, so I'm going to go do what everyone else is too afraid to try."

She looks at me with an intensity that makes me want to turn away, as if she's seeing something deeper than I'm willing to show. "You're wrong again," she says softly, reaching out to grab my hand. I instantly feel a spark between us, the physical reminder of how strong our magic becomes when we're together.

"You feel it, too, right?" she confirms. "You and I are linked, whether you like it or not. You are one of my Four, and I do need you.

I don't know what's going to happen next, but I know that all our plans will fail without you here.

"And what about Permiton?" I ask, though I immediately regret it when I see her face fall.

"What about him," she asks quietly, her expression wounded. "I was clearly wrong about him."

"So how do you know that you weren't wrong about me?" I argue. "You were so desperate to find your Four, to save your kingdom, but what if I'm not one of them?"

"Of course, you're one of them!" she shouts, losing her temper. She slams into me, kissing me hard, and my whole body feels the surge of power. She pulls away quickly. "That is how I know. So, yes, I need you."

My chest tightens at her words, and for a moment, I feel something other than the frustration that's been eating away at me. There's warmth in her eyes, a sincerity that makes me feel like maybe there's a place for me here after all.

I swallow, struggling to find the right words. "I just want to do something that matters, Maerilee. I want to prove that I'm not just someone to keep around out of pity. Or obligation."

She squeezes my arm, her gaze warm. There's no trace of pity or ire, just sincere concern. "I'm so sorry that I've neglected you, Brook," she answers quietly. "You're here because I need you, and I should have been clearer about that. I know that I always run to Akin for comfort, but you have to understand the deep history between us. He's been my guard, my protector, for as long as I can remember. Even before all of this, we had a friendship. I trust him. But I trust you, too, and I'm sorry that I haven't done a good job of showing it."

The weight on my chest eases, replaced by a strange mix of relief and something I can't quite name. She sees me. She needs me. And in that moment, the urge to run fades, replaced by a quiet determination to stay, to prove that I can be the person she believes I am.

But then another thought occurs. We could run away together. I could be the one to bring her to Bright Waters. The others would be furious, I'm sure, but if I could deliver her there, to bring her the cure for her mother's ailment, she'd see how much I care about her, how much I'm willing to do for her. I'm about to open my mouth to speak when a raven circles overhead, dropping a small rock so close to us that it only nearly misses her head.

We both look up, and I catch sight of the bird, its feathers glossy and dark as night, landing gracefully on a nearby rock. It tilts its head, almost as if it's studying us, and then gracefully swoops down toward us, dropping a small piece of parchment at Maerilee's feet.

She bends down, picking up the note, and I can see the hesitation in her eyes as she unfolds it. Her face goes pale as her eyes scan the words, and a shiver of dread runs down my spine.

"What is it?" I ask curiously, my voice barely above a whisper. "What does it say?"

"It's from Permiton," she answers, her breath hitching.

10

ANOTHER PERSPECTIVE

PERMITON

Several Days Ago

We stand on the edge of the shoreline, and the visions attack me, sharp and violent. Each image is simply a possibility, a road that will unfurl depending on what decision we make. River and Brook stand by the water, each trying to conjure a narwhal-pulled ferry, but they're wasting their energy. It will not come for them; they've been exiled. The moment the decree was made, every living organism in this country turned against them.

The army wants their blood, that much is clear. When the princes stepped over the border, the army was alerted of their presence. They're coming, no matter what we do. That is the only certainty in our future. The rest is up to us to decide.

The boys, the princes, will fight. That's what they know to do. I can see it all unfurl, the way they summon all their strength and fight off the soldiers with their water magic. They're impressive, I can't fault them that, but they're arrogant. River, especially, still thinks that his title of prince still means something. He has yet to fully grasp the implications of his exile. He'll know soon enough. The commander of the army will kill him first, slit his throat just for the glory of it.

Of course, Commander Heela can't possibly know what a relief that would be to us. River might be one of Maerilee's Four, but he's by far the least favorite. It's one of the only things we all agree on. His death would have no impact, not even on his brother.

But, the commander could also change his mind and kill Brook first. Strangely, that would enrage River much more than River's death would affect Brook. River will go out swinging, fighting for vengeance for his brother. He'll easily be slain, of course. What is one man against an army?

For maximum impact, though, Heela will have to decide to kill Akin first. That vision solidifies for me, and it will for the man if he sees them together long enough to understand their connection. He knows about Maerilee, of course. When he comes ashore, he'll call her a freak. It isn't her fault that she was given this burden, but he won't see it that way. The Oceaneans aren't like the Altinnians. Their customs seem foreign and strange.

So, if Heela is given any chance to see how much Akin and Maerilee care about each other, he'll kill Akin first. Akin is a strong fighter. He won't be taken down easily. But that's what will make it all the more satisfying. Commander Heela is an evil man, his heart as black as a starless night. He's racing toward us to put an end to this, what he calls, depraved madness. If we try to hide, to flee back to Altinna, he'll take pleasure in bringing down the barrier earlier.

We are out of options.

Then there are his plans for Maerilee. He doesn't know which of us men he'll kill first, but he's going to make her suffer. He's already decided on the most vile, depraved punishment for her, and he intends to keep her as his slave for years. He will break her, turn her into an unrecognizable shell of herself.

I cannot let that happen. I am the only one who can make a decision to save us. I'm the only unknown variable.

So I'll have to betray them. It's the only way to keep them safe. The moment I decide it, I can see the path unfurl before me, as if I could step through and walk down it. If I betray them, pretend that I've brought them to the commander as a gift, he will reward me. They'll be uncomfortable for a few days, but Commander Heela doesn't know he has enemies here. They're Altinnian.

Their leader is named Caelan, and he already knows that we've arrived, too. He has spies all over the kingdom. But he's too far to reach us here. He's no good to us on the shore, so we'll have to cross the lake and start the journey to the castle. I must convince Heela of this. His prize will be much greater when he delivers them to the king and queen. He'll be rewarded, lauded.

Of course, he won't make it that far. The rebels will attack in the forest, save the others, and get them to safety. In the meantime, I will use him, collect all the knowledge about Bright Waters I need, and slip away when the moment is right. Maerilee will be angry, I see that clear as day. But she will eventually forgive me once she knows the truth.

Sure enough, the Oceanean army comes ashore. My early betrayal of the group makes Commander Heela think I'm on his side. He allows his soldiers to fight, but he sees the wisdom in not killing them yet.

The fight goes on, my companions wearing themselves out until the soldiers easily overtake them. I move to stand by the commander, carefully avoiding the fight. If this is going to work, I must keep my wits about me.

"Permiton!" Maerilee screams out, her voice broken and defeated. "Why are you doing this?"

One day she'll understand. She'll be glad that I did this. So I don't let her emotion concern me.

"Because it's what's necessary," I tell her quietly, hoping my words will convey the truth of the situation.

* * *

Last Night

Heela's been agitated since the rebels infiltrated the camp. His search for my companions grows more dire as his anger multiplies.

His efforts will, of course, be fruitless. As long as my companions decide to head for Bright Waters, all will go according to the path.

The commander's tent is dimly lit, illuminated only by a few lanterns that flicker against the fabric walls. I keep my expression neutral as he studies me, his eyes full of skepticism laced with just enough interest to keep me on edge. There's a map spread across his table, the familiar contours of Altinna marked in precise lines, arrows, and positions drawn around it like a game of conquest. They've laid out every strategic detail of their coming attack, and now I know their plans.

"Permiton," Heela begins, his tone low, as though he's weighing my worth with each syllable, "you've proved useful so far, but I'm not convinced of your motives. You've betrayed your kingdom for Altinna and your little freak show for us. What do you get from this?"

I pause, carefully calculating my response. "I'm only loyal to myself," I tell him, knowing that's an answer he'll respect. "Altinna has lost its strength, its power. It's only a matter of time before it falls. If I can benefit from that fall, if I can carve out a place for myself when it's all over, that's all I need."

It's a lie, but it's conniving enough to sound plausible. Heela's gaze doesn't waver, but he gives a curt nod, turning his attention back to the map. I keep my face impassive, watching as he marks their planned routes and strategizes the positions of his forces.

I've nearly memorized the map now, the image seared into my brain. If nothing else, I can use this information to regain my companions' trust. I'm so focused on the task, I don't hear the sound of heavy boots approaching.

"Well, well, if it isn't the esteemed Permiton, once again blending in where he doesn't belong."

I turn, the blood draining from my face as I recognize the voice. Diereken strides into the tent, his expression a mix of amusement and malice. His gaze lingers on me, and I know in that instant that my cover is blown.

Heela's head snaps up, his eyes narrowing.

Diereken, my friend," he greets him, standing up and shaking the filthy prince's hand. "You know my new weapon?"

"Oh, I know him all too well," Diereken replies, a dangerous smirk twisting his mouth. "He once belonged to my kingdom, but he defected to that hedonistic kingdom of Altinna. He's part of the princess's disgusting harem."

I should have seen this coming, should have realized that Diereken would have shown up here. I curse the holes in my Sight, my arrogance in thinking Diereken would go back to Ambrosia. I should have anticipated his alliance with the Oceaneans.

Commander Heela's face contorts with fury as he turns to me, hand already moving to the hilt of his sword. I take a step back, my fingers itching toward my own blade, but I know I'm outnumbered, outmatched. There's no way I can fight my way out of this.

I need to run. Now.

Without waiting another second, I whirl around, darting toward the entrance of the tent. Shouts echo behind me, the scrape of metal and the sudden rush of footsteps signaling that they're right on my heels. I push forward, my heart pounding as I race through the camp, weaving between tents and soldiers, every instinct screaming at me to move faster, to get out before it's too late.

The world blurs as I sprint into the forest, the shadows swallowing me up as I slip into the cover of the trees. The sounds of pursuit fade behind me, but I know they won't give up that easily. I've seen the ruthlessness of the Oceanean forces firsthand, and they'll hunt me until they're sure I'm dead. In my mind, I see the commander beheading me, showing off my head as a prize. I won't let it get that far.

Thankfully, my Sight has given me a path through the forest, one the Oceaneans don't know about. It's one Caelan has mapped out, his forces becoming better acquainted with this terrain than the locals. I flee into the night, not slowing until I'm sure I've put at least half a day's space between myself and the army. It's a narrow window of escape, but it's enough to find my companions and get to Bright Waters. After that, everything changes.

As I stop to catch my breath, I reach into my coat pocket, pulling out a small piece of parchment and a quill. I quickly scratch out a hasty message to Maerilee then slip it in my pocket and continue my travel. I see a vision of Heela as clear as day, his fury so severe I can almost feel it myself. He's redoubling his efforts to find us all, but at least now his attention is split.

I keep moving, not daring to stop fully just yet. I find a clearing and hold the parchment out to a raven, murmuring instructions as it flaps its wings, taking flight and disappearing into the night. I can only hope it reaches them in time. I hope that Maerilee will read it, that she'll understand why I had to do what I did.

Once the Raven disappears, I press forward, my body moving on instinct. I don't know where Maerilee and the others are exactly, but I know where they're going. As long as one of them decides to leave the rebels for Bright Waters, I will be able to find them there.

I begin my ascent into the mountains knowing I'll have to climb up a steep cliff if I have any chance of making it in time. They're quickly going to realize that they can't enter Bright Waters without me, so I have to be prepared to arrive at just the right moment.

11

ALL IS NOT LOST

Maerilee

THE MESSAGE FEELS WEIGHTY IN MY HANDS AS I READ IT, EACH WORD burrowing into my mind, stirring a confusing blend of relief and uncertainty. Permiton has tried, on a very small parchment of paper, to explain his version of events. He's written about why he turned against us, how he saw a vision of our destruction and had to make a quick decision, how there was no time to explain.

In a few short words, he tries to convey that we can still trust him, that he would never truly betray us. Even still, I feel the urge to crush the paper in my fist, to rid myself of the tangled emotions twisting inside me, but instead, I reach for Brook, who's been sitting nearby, quietly watching, waiting. I need him to read this, to make sense of it with me.

"It's from Permiton," I say, holding the note out to him. "I'm not sure what to make of it."

He takes it carefully, his brow furrowing as his eyes scan over Permiton's handwriting. His silence stretches, and I feel the pressure building as I wait. When he finally looks up, his face holds something I can't read, something deep and contemplative.

"Do you believe him?" I ask, my voice barely above a whisper, almost afraid of the answer. "Do you believe any of this?"

He lets out a slow breath, folding the paper gently as he gathers his thoughts.

"I don't know what to think, Maerilee," he says finally, his voice soft but steady. "Right now, these are just words. His actions are going to have to prove them. But I do believe one thing. Whatever else is true or false, I know that the Bright Waters are real."

His words catch me off guard, a spark of hope igniting within me, despite everything. For the last several days, I've been so certain that all hope was lost. Now, he's telling me that we're not on a hopeless mission, that Mother can be saved after all.

"How can you be so sure?" I say, my voice hardly above a whisper as I try to process his words.

He hesitates, glancing down at his hands before meeting my eyes again. "My family had stories," he begins, his eyes going distant as he remembers the past. "Old, secret stories, ones we weren't supposed to speak of. My father once told me about the Bright Waters, how they were the strongest magic in the entire realm. He said they were a source of great power, that they'd been hidden away to protect them from those who would use them for destruction. If I have even a chance to bring you there, I'll do it. I'd do anything to make sure you reach them and get what you need."

I stare at him, the sincerity in his voice resonating in ways I hadn't expected. Brook, who's been so uncertain, so withdrawn, so insecure, now stands before me, pledging himself to this journey with a conviction that nearly takes my breath away.

"I–" I falter, searching for words, the conflicting thoughts in my mind fighting for dominance.

Akin believes Caelan, and I've always trusted Akin's judgment. But as I look into his eyes, into the unshakable certainty there, I realize what I want and need is clear.

"We'll go then," I say, the decision solidifying within me even as I speak it. "Even if it's just you and me. If we have to, we'll break free of the others and make our way there."

A faint smile tugs at Brook's lips, and I feel a warmth settle between us, a quiet understanding that, for the first time, feels unbreakable.

"Are you sure?" he asks, his usual self-consciousness returning underneath his excitement. "It's a big decision to go, Maerilee. No one will miss me, but we're all here for you. If you disappear, they'll do everything they can to find you."

I process his words, and I realize the risk that I'm opening myself up to. Running away, leaving Akin, River, and even Caelan, will undoubtedly create complications. Brook is right. They'll come looking for us. Brook is so sure that Bright Waters is real, though, and if they do decide to come with us, we'll have more backup for whatever tasks await.

A shiver runs through me, one of excitement and a little fear. I don't know what the road to Bright Waters will entail, but I know it will be dangerous. My powers will be weakened even further without the others, but I know that Brook isn't going to let me down. Despite his lack of self-confidence, he's shown impressive magical abilities. If need be, I believe that the two of us can make it.

"Brook," I say softly, glancing around to make sure no one's found us, "there's something I need to know. Do you trust Caelan?"

Brook's expression hardens, his usual gentle features sharpening with something darker. "I don't," he says firmly. "He seems to say all the right things to gain Akin's trust and even yours. But there's something off about him. I don't know what it is, but it's enough to make me wary. He's been in this kingdom a long time, yet he doubts the reality of our most sacred and powerful source of magic. Maybe he's too blinded by his allegiance to Altinna to truly embrace the truth."

I let out a shaky breath, a sense of validation washing over me. Brook's doubt mirrors my own, though I'd been hesitant to acknowledge it before because Akin was so certain of Caelan. It's hard not to trust someone who claims to be an ally, someone who's helped us, who's theoretically guiding us to safety. But deep down, I never trusted that what he said about Bright Waters is true. How could I? It's the only way I can save my mother.

"We should plan to leave as soon as possible," I say, feeling the words solidify my decision. "Tonight, if we can. Once everyone else is asleep, we'll sneak away and try to put as much distance between us and them as possible."

Brook nods, and we fall silent, a heavy atmosphere growing between us. I haven't been alone with him much since our journey began, and I can understand his frustration and his desire to leave on his own. I shouldn't have been so flippant with his feelings. Everyone in his life has seemed to overlook him, and I'd promised myself that I wouldn't be one of them when we met.

"Brook," I say quietly, forcing him to look at me. He meets my gaze hesitantly, perhaps worried that I've already changed my mind. "Thank you for confiding in me. And I'm sorry if you've felt that I've overlooked you. That was never my intention. You're just as important to this mission as anyone else."

He nods slowly, and I notice a tinge of red beginning to color his cheeks. But I realize that I haven't conveyed the fullness of my appreciation for him. He is one of my Four, a piece of the puzzle that makes me whole. Never once has he given me a reason to doubt him, and his steadfastness has been a gift through these trying times.

"Truthfully, Brook, you're just as important to me," I amend quietly, placing my hand on his cheek and feeling the growing warmth there.

He looks into my eyes, his expression slightly guarded, but hopeful. I lean in closer to him, closing the distance between us until our bodies are flush against each other. His arms move to my waist, holding me there as if he's afraid I'll disappear. I have no plans of going anywhere, though, and my hands curl around his neck, my fingers gripping his hair slightly to show him that I'm as in this as he is.

He bends down slowly, gently, until he's just a breath away. Even here, in the intimacy of our embrace, he acts unsure, hesitant. But I don't want him to ever feel fear with me, to ever think that I don't want him or that he's just a second, third, or fourth choice. He's so easy to be around, so sweet and so patient.

I erase all the space between us, meeting his slightly parted lips with my own, kissing him with a certainty and assuredness to let him know that I'm not hesitant about him. If there's one thing I trust, it's that Brook is never going to let me down. It's time to stop letting him down.

I slide my hands down his neck, dragging them slowly down his chest and eliciting a soft groan of pleasure. My hands fiddle with the hem of his shirt, slowly pulling it up his body to reveal the hardness of his abs and chest.

His body is exquisite, something I've forgotten in the midst of all the chaos of the last several days. A surge of heat begins pooling between my legs, and I want him desperately. I'm aching for him, I realize.

He lifts his arms above his head as I push his shirt away, throwing it on the mossy ground.

"I need you," I whisper desperately, unashamed of the desire dripping from my words. "Right now."

He smiles and looks around us, trying to decide what to do.

"I don't mind a little dirt," I whisper huskily before sinking down to the soft earth and pulling him with me, on top of me.

He carefully balances above me, his weight on one elbow as his other hand moves to the hem of my skirts. His lips meet mine again, urgent, hungry, and sloppy. I feel the warmth of his hand teasing up my leg, setting trails of fire everywhere he touches.

A branch snaps somewhere nearby, and we both freeze, suddenly remembering where we are and that anyone could come upon us. In the haze of our lust, we'd both forgotten. I look at Brook slightly panicked because no part of me wants to stop.

We wait breathlessly, but when no one appears, Brook erects a barrier of water around us, shielding us from anyone who might wander upon us. With that taken care of, his hand finds my center, already wet and warm for him, eager for his touch.

As his fingers brush against me, my hips buck of their own accord, one hand tangling so tightly in his hair that he hisses and tries to pull away.

"Sorry," I murmur with some embarrassment, loosening my grip just a little.

He smiles, but his lips don't meet mine again. Instead, he trains his eyes on me. They're dark, dangerous, completely unguarded.

His fingers slip inside of me slowly, and I suddenly realize what it is he wants. He wants to watch me as I fall apart. Something about his sudden shift, his willingness to take charge, is so alluring to me. I watch him through hooded eyes, biting my lip as he continues his movements.

As his thumb brushes over my clit, my eyes roll into the back of my head, and I begin to see stars forming at the edge of my consciousness. But it isn't enough. With my eyes still slightly closed, I release him from my grasp, trailing my hands down his body until I find the clasp of his trousers.

"Maerilee," he warns in a low voice, the huskiness of his voice sending a spark of electricity through me.

"I want all of you," I respond, opening my eyes to meet his gaze.

He nods quickly as I unsheathe him.

He removes his hand from me slowly, pushing my skirts further up so that he has better access. With a quick, confident move, he aligns himself perfectly to me, his hardness filing me completely. The move is so sudden, I lose my breath for a moment, slamming my eyes shut again as I get lost in the sensation.

He stops for a moment, asks me if I'm okay. I can only nod, my hands moving back to his face as I pull him back down to kiss me deeply.

1 2

BREAKING OF RANKS

Maerilee approaches me with a tension in her step that I don't miss. Her shoulders are squared, her expression guarded, and there's a fire in her eyes that instantly puts me on alert.

"There you are," I call out happily, hoping to break the tension a bit. "I was wondering where you'd run off to."

"Akin," she says, her voice calm but with an edge I've rarely heard before. "We need to talk."

My stomach drops. I'm suddenly afraid of what she might say. Our relationship has always been easy and light. Though I yearned for her in so many secret ways, there was never such a high wall between us as there is right now. My mind races just imagining what horrible information she feels she must tell me.

I cross my arms, giving her a small nod, expecting the worst. Perhaps she's received word from home somehow. My suspicion is increased when she pulls a note from the folds of her dress and hands it to me, her expression serious.

"Read it," she says, watching me closely.

I take the note and unfold it, my eyes scanning over the words. Once I see the signature at the bottom, I have to read it several more times to fully understand. It's a warning, a plea, a flimsy explanation for his actions. He claims he's coming, that he didn't betray us, and that we need to listen to him if we want to survive. The words feel hollow, like a badly rehearsed excuse. I crumple the parchment in my fist, barely restraining my anger.

"You can't be serious," I say, my voice hard. "After everything he's done, he thinks a few words scrawled quickly on a piece of paper will change our minds about him? He's absolutely unbelievable."

Her face remains steady, though I catch a flicker of something behind her eyes.

"I believe him," she says simply, causing a pang of betrayal to shoot through my chest. "Permiton made mistakes, yes. But he's trying to help us now."

"Help us?" I nearly spit it out. I can barely contain my frustration now, though I don't want to take it out on her. "The man's reason for betrayal is only as good as his word, and right now, his word means nothing. After what we were put through, he doesn't have the right to tell us it was for our own good."

Her eyes immediately drop to my wrists, and I can still feel the sting of the ropes, though the pain has worn off from Caelan's salve.

She takes a steadying breath, her gaze wary. It hurts me to see her this way, to realize that she's being hesitant with me. She's holding back from me, and it stings more than the ropes ever could.

"Akin, this isn't just about Permiton," she responds calmly, taking a steadying breath and sitting down on a nearby log. I sit next to her and wait patiently for her explanation. "It's about finding the Bright Waters," she eventually says, meeting my gaze with a heartbreaking sadness. "My mother's life depends on it."

"You think I don't care about your mother?" My voice rises, and I can see the flash of surprise in her eyes at the intensity. "I would do anything for her. For you. But Bright Waters is a fairytale, Maerilee. I know you want to believe in it, but Caelan says it doesn't exist, and I believe him. He's one of us. He has no reason to lie to us."

Her mouth sets in a tight line, her jaw clenched. "So, what then? You think it's better to stay here, to fight alongside rebels we barely know, following Caelan's every move? You think that's going to save Altinna? If my mother dies, the barrier will fall, and all will be lost. And I'll never be able to re-erect the barrier without Permiton!"

I sigh in frustration, looking up to the lightening sky for hope that it will bring me some kind of clarity. Why is she being like this? We were on the same page earlier, but suddenly, her mind has changed. How can she possibly trust Permiton this much after what he did to us?

"What is this really about, Maerilee?" I whisper, taking her hand in mine.

She meets my gaze with the warmth I'm more accustomed to, but she pulls her hand away and balls it into a fist. "I don't trust Caelan," she finally whispers, looking around us to make sure she isn't overheard. "You're right. He has no reason to lie to us, and still, I think he's wrong about Bright Waters. Brook believes that it exists, and I'm inclined to believe him. This is his home. He would know better than anyone."

"It's not his home anymore," I argue, though a sinking feeling begins to settle in my stomach. She seems to have made up her mind without me.

"Then what do you suggest?" she asks, a sharp edge to her voice. "Are we just supposed to follow Caelan blindly and hope that everything turns out okay?"

"It's a better plan than running after a legend!" The words come out sharper than I intended, but I don't hold them back. "Caelan's strategy makes sense. He's organized, and his men are ready. We could make a difference here, protect you, and ensure Altinna has the allies it needs."

"But what good is that if my mother dies before we get back?" Her voice cracks, and for a moment, I see the fear beneath her defiance. "If there's even the slightest chance that Bright Waters is real, that it could save her, then why wouldn't we take it?"

I open my mouth, but no words come out. She's looking at me with an intensity I can't bear, as though searching for something I can't give her. Because, as much as I want to believe, as much as I want to be the one she can rely on, I can't lead her on with false hopes. I can't lie to her, even if it's what she wants to hear.

"I would give anything," I say quietly, my voice barely more than a whisper. "Anything. But this, chasing after something that isn't real, it's a waste, Maerilee. I'm trying to protect you."

"Protect me?" she echoes sarcastically, anger flashing in her eyes. "By keeping me from doing the one thing that might actually save my mother? Or is this just about you wanting to be in charge?"

The accusation hits me like a punch to the gut, and I move away from her, stunned. But before I can respond, we're interrupted by the sound of footsteps. River and Brook appear from around the corner, their faces set in matching expressions of determination and caution.

River gives me a once-over, his eyes narrowing as he takes in the tension. "What's going on?" he asks, crossing his arms as he looks between us.

"Permiton has sent us a note," Maerilee says, holding it out. "Akin doesn't think we should trust him or go after the Bright Waters. He wants us to stay here with Caelan."

River lets out a low chuckle, a smirk playing at the corners of his mouth. "Well, I hate to agree with Akin on anything, but he's not wrong to question Permiton's loyalty."

"But he is wrong about the Bright Waters," Brook says, his tone soft but unwavering. He meets my gaze, and I can see the conviction in his eyes, the belief I've struggled to find within myself. "They're real, Akin. I know it."

"Brook," I begin, feeling the familiar frustration rise within me. "You don't—"

"I do know," he says, cutting me off, his voice firmer than I've ever heard it. "My family's stories weren't just fairytales. They were truths passed down, kept safe. My father knew about the Bright Waters, about their power. And I'm not going to sit here and ignore that."

I glance between them, feeling the ground shift beneath me. Three against one. Four if you count Permiton's damned note. Every instinct in me screams to push back, to argue, but the look in Maerilee's eyes holds me back. There's a quiet desperation there, a vulnerability that makes me falter, even though everything in me wants to fight against this.

"Maerilee," I say, my voice strained. "You trust this? You trust that Permiton, of all people, is leading us the right way?"

She stands up, closing the distance between us, her hand finding mine, her touch grounding me, steadying me even as my thoughts spin out of control. "I trust you, Akin. But I know this is the right move. I can feel it. And I want you to come with me. But I will go without you if you don't believe in this."

The sincerity in her words, the unwavering belief in her voice, makes something inside me crack. I've fought so hard to protect her, to keep her safe, but maybe I've been so focused on my role that I've forgotten what she needs most right now.

I nod, letting out a long breath as I meet her gaze. "I'll follow you to the ends of the earth," I promise, squeezing her hand. "Whatever happens, I'll be there."

Relief softens her features, a small smile tugging at her lips as she squeezes my hand. It's a moment of quiet understanding, of shared trust that feels like a balm after the unexpected spat we just had. I might not believe in the Bright Waters, but I believe in her. And if this is what she needs, if this is the path she's chosen, then I'll be by her side.

We start gathering our things, moving as quickly and quietly as we can so we don't rouse suspicion from the rebels. But just as we're about to take our leave of the camp, a figure steps into our path, his presence as solid and unyielding as the mountains around us.

Caelan.

His eyes narrow as he takes in the scene, the packed bags, the determined set of Maerilee's jaw. "Going somewhere?" he asks, his tone deceptively calm.

I step forward, instinctively moving between him and Maerilee. "We're leaving," I say firmly, meeting his gaze without wavering. "There's something we need to do."

Caelan crosses his arms, a glint of suspicion flickering in his eyes.

"I thought we had an agreement, Akin. I thought we were fighting together."

"We are," I reply, though the words feel hollow. "But this is something Maerilee needs to do. We don't need your help for this."

He glances over my shoulder, his gaze settling on Maerilee.

She steps forward, her voice steady and unwavering. "My mother needs the Bright Waters, and I believe they exist. As her proxy in this land, I am telling you that we're leaving. You don't have to like it, but you will respect my decision."

For a moment, Caelan simply stares at her, his expression unreadable. Then he lets out a soft sigh, a hint of something almost like disappointment flashing across his face.

"I thought we were working toward the same goal. But it seems your faith lies elsewhere."

I can feel the tension growing between us, and my hand instinctively tightens around my sword, ready to step between the two of them if things get out of control. I like Caelan, sincerely. He's been a brother in arms the last few days, and that's been a nice feeling after being in the company of Maerilee's other Three.

But my loyalty is and always will be to her, and I won't let him stand in the way. The choice before me is clear. I will protect her. Always.

13

FLIGHT INTO THE MOUNTAINS

Akin

CAELAN STANDS IN FRONT OF US, HIS GAZE HARD AS STEEL, JAW
clenched, and I know instantly that this won't end with us simply
walking away. The way he's squared his shoulders, planted his feet,
every muscle in his body is telling me he won't let us leave without a
fight.

And I don't want to fight him. Not here, not now, when we're all
running on fumes and tensions are high enough to snap. But there's
something militant, almost desperate, in his stance. It's the way he'd
face an enemy, and it feels wrong. We're supposed to be allies, yet
here we are, at a breaking point.

"Caelan," I say, forcing my tone to stay calm. "Let us go. This isn't
about abandoning the cause or betraying the rebels. Maerilee needs
this. Altinna needs this."

Caelan's eyes flash, the determination in them blazing. "And what
do you think we're doing here, Akin? We're building a force strong
enough to defend Altinna. Leaving now will unravel all the ground-

work we've laid. I don't care what stories you're chasing. You leave, and you're on your own."

His words hit hard, but I don't flinch. "I understand your loyalty, Caelan. I respect it. But this isn't your choice to make."

"Not my choice?" He steps forward, anger flickering across his face. "You're turning your back on a rebellion we need to strengthen Altinna's defenses. Every one of you is part of this. I'm not letting you walk away just because you've decided some myth is worth more than the people here."

I can feel the heat rising, frustration clawing at me, but I hold my ground. Before I have a chance to retort, though, Brook, of all people, steps up and speaks out.

"It's not a myth, Caelan," he says with more confidence than I knew he was capable of. "The Bright Waters are real. They could be the only thing that saves Queen Kimalissa."

"And what if they're not?" Caelan counters, his voice tight. "You're gambling with lives, and I won't let you. We stay together, and we fight as one. No more division in the ranks."

He's rigid, unyielding, and a familiar weight settles in my gut. It's the same feeling I get right before a confrontation. But as I shift my stance, readying for the inevitable clash, I see Maerilee out of the corner of my eye. Her face is drawn with worry, and I realize that a fight here will only add to her burden, to the already impossible weight she's carrying.

"Caelan," I say, softer now, hoping to reach him beneath the anger. "This isn't just about us. It's about Altinna's survival. You're a good leader, a strong leader, but you have to trust that we know what we're doing. Maerilee knows what she's doing."

He shakes his head, his grip tightening on the hilt of his weapon. "Trust doesn't protect people, Akin. Actions do."

I take a step back, fists clenched, heart pounding with a mixture of anger and frustration. I can see the division widening between us, feel the weight of it pressing down. This isn't the way I wanted it to go.

"You have a choice here, Caelan. All you have to do is let us leave. I don't want to fight you. That won't help anyone."

His expression hardens, and I see the flicker of decision in his eyes, a readiness to fight, to force us to stay. I brace myself, preparing for the confrontation I've tried so hard to avoid.

But before either of us can move, a commotion breaks out in the trees. Footsteps pound against the ground, and a group of Caelan's scouts burst into the clearing, their faces pale, eyes wide with urgency.

"Commander!" one of them shouts, breathless and panicked. "The Oceanean army's found us. They're right on our heels."

Caelan stiffens, his focus shifting from us to the scouts, a quick calculation flashing in his eyes. "How close?"

The scout swallows, glancing nervously over his shoulder. "Minutes away. We have to leave. Now."

For a moment, everything hangs in the balance. Caelan's jaw tightens, his gaze flicking between me, Maerilee, and the scouts, the weight of the situation pressing down on him. I see the conflict in his eyes, the struggle to hold onto control, even as the reality of our situation looms over him.

"Fine," he snaps, his tone edged with frustration. "Everyone, gather what you can and move out. Now."

He turns away, barking orders to his men, the tension still crackling in the air between us. The moment feels heavy, unresolved, but there's no time to dwell on it. I motion to Maerilee, River, and Brook, and we quickly grab our things, running in the opposite direction of the rebels.

The atmosphere is charged, every face tense, every movement filled with urgency. The Oceanean army is closing in, and whatever divisions we have or arguments and anger still simmering are forced to the back of our minds. Survival takes precedence, and in that shared purpose, a fragile, temporary truce settles over us.

As we move through the dense undergrowth, following Brook's lead, I find myself falling into step beside Maerilee. Her face is pale but determined, her jaw set in that stubborn line I know so well. I reach out, giving her shoulder a quick, reassuring squeeze. She glances at me, and despite everything, I see a flicker of gratitude in her eyes.

"Don't be afraid, my love," I murmur, keeping my voice low. "Just stay close. We'll get through this together."

She nods, her gaze steady. "Thank you, Akin. For everything."

We press on, the sounds of the Oceanean army growing louder behind us, the tension building with each step. The trees grow denser, the undergrowth thicker, and our pace slows as we navigate the increasingly treacherous terrain. Every step feels like a gamble, every sound a potential threat. The Oceaneans are close–too close–and the weight of their presence presses down on us like a dark, looming shadow.

The path narrows, forcing us to move in single file. We eventually break through a dense thicket, emerging onto a rocky outcrop that overlooks the forest below. Brook halts, glancing around, his gaze sharp as he assesses the terrain. He's looking for the next move, the best way to get away from the Oceaneans without alerting him to our presence.

"Down there," he says, pointing to a narrow path that winds along the edge of the cliffs. "It's dangerous, but it'll buy us time. We can lose them in the rocks."

The others nod, and we quickly move toward the path, slipping into the shadows cast by the towering cliffs. Every step echoes against the walls of stone.

Maerilee

THE SOUNDS OF CHAOS SWIRL ON THE CLIFFS ABOVE US. WE HEAR THE sounds of shouts, the clash of weapons, the frenzied rustling of underbrush as everyone scrambles to find a way out.

Caelan's voice can be heard faintly in the distance, his orders ringing out above the fray, sharp and insistent, but they blend with the cries of his soldiers as they clash with the Oceaneans. The trees seem to close in around us, thick and tangled, blocking out the light and swallowing up the noise in a suffocating cloak of shadow and confusion.

Even so, I'm grateful to Brook for leading us away so efficiently. He's already proven his strength tenfold, and I know he's going to get us to Bright Waters safely. We just have to get away from the rebels and the army as quickly and carefully as we can.

I take a steadying breath, focusing my energy. I don't have much power without Permiton's presence nearby, but I have enough, a small reservoir of magic I can tap into. It's just enough to keep us hidden, to shield us from the eyes and ears of those around us. I focus on that power, feeling it settle around us like a thin veil, shimmering and fragile but effective enough to keep us unnoticed in the chaos.

"Stay close," I whisper, reaching out to River, Brook, and Akin, drawing them into a tight circle. "I'll shield us, but we have to move quickly and quietly. The Oceanean army can't see us, or we're dead."

River's eyes narrow, his usual smug expression replaced by a look of determination. Brook gives me a slight nod, his face calm, resolved. Akin's gaze meets mine, a flicker of understanding passing between us. He chose his side, and I can see that same fierce protectiveness in his expression, the same willingness to follow me wherever this road might lead.

We slip into the shadows, my shield surrounding us like a thin mist, barely visible but enough to make us fade into the dense forest. I keep one hand outstretched, letting my magic pulse through me, guiding us deeper into the mountains, away from the battlefield, away from Caelan and his men, away from certain death.

As we move, the sounds of battle begin to fade, the distant shouts and ricocheting metal growing muffled by the trees, replaced by the quieter rustle of leaves, the soft crunch of pine needles beneath our feet. The air grows colder, crisper as we climb higher into the mountains.

"Are you sure you're strong enough for this?" Akin's concerned voice breaks through the silence, low and cautious.

I glance back at him, meeting his gaze with as much confidence as I can muster. "I'll be fine. We just need to put as much space between the battle and ourselves as possible. Then, I can put the shield down."

He nods, though I can see the doubt flicker in his eyes, his concern evident. But he doesn't question me further. Instead, he falls in line behind me, his presence a steady reassurance.

Brook and River follow close behind, each of them silent, their expressions tense but determined. I can feel the weight of their trust, the unspoken understanding that we're all bound to this path now, that there's no turning back. And for the first time since we started this journey, I feel a strange sense of unity between us, a shared purpose that cuts through the lingering doubts, the fear that has haunted me.

We continue moving deeper into the dense forest, the mountain looming above us, its rocky cliffs casting long shadows that stretch like fingers across our path. The air grows colder still, the trees thickening, their branches interwoven like a labyrinth that blocks out the sky. My shield flickers, the strain of holding it up alone pressing down on me, but I push through, focusing on the rhythm of our footsteps, the steady pulse of magic that guides us forward.

A flash of movement catches my eye, and I turn, my heart pounding, but it's only a shadow, a trick of the dim light. I release a shaky breath, my nerves fraying as we press on, every rustle, every snap of a twig setting my heart racing.

Finally, we reach a small clearing, the ground sloping up toward a narrow ridge that winds further into the mountains. I lower my hand, letting the shield dissolve, and we pause, catching our breath, the silence of the forest pressing down around us.

"Where to now?" River asks, his voice surprisingly devoid of any hint of derision.

I glance around, the unfamiliar landscape stretching out before us like a maze, each path twisting and turning, leading deeper into the wilderness. I wish I knew for certain, wish I could sense the Bright Waters, could feel their pull, but all I have is the faintest hint of direction, a whisper in my mind that nudges me forward.

"We're headed in the right direction," Brook affirms, grabbing my hand and squeezing it gently. "We should be there within a few hours."

River scoffs, crossing his arms. "When did you grow a pair of balls? Who put you in charge, anyway?"

I shoot him a glare, my patience fraying. "If it weren't for Brook, we'd probably be back with the rebels fighting for our lives. It was his certainty that convinced me we should leave. I trust that he knows where he's going, and it's about time you give him the respect he deserves."

He holds my gaze for a moment, his expression unreadable, but then he lets out a sigh, nodding and turning to Brook. "Fine. Lead the way, brother."

I turn, feeling a surge of relief and determination, and we begin moving again, weaving through the trees, following the path that twists and turns up the mountainside. The air grows thinner, sharper, each breath coming harder as we climb, but we press on, my focus narrowing to the steady rhythm of our footsteps, the faint pulse of magic that guides me.

Hours pass, the forest growing darker, the shadows stretching longer as the sun dips behind the mountains. My legs ache, my energy waning, but I push through, the weight of our purpose driving me forward.

14

THE WEIGHT OF UNBEARABLE TENSION

Maerilee

THE SILENCE BETWEEN US IS PALPABLE, AS IF EVERYONE IS HOLDING their tongue but projecting their thoughts to the clouds. No one is willing to break the silence, to put their thoughts to words, and it's becoming infuriating.

I worry that Akin is still angry with me, despite his stance to leave Caelan and travel with us. River is smug, as usual, though I have no idea what he could be thinking. Brook leads us with confidence and certainty, and while I don't doubt him, it's clear that Akin and River do.

I glance at Akin, hoping to find some sign of reassurance, something to tell me that all is forgiven. But his face is closed off, his jaw clenched as he stares straight ahead, shoulders rigid. I don't need words to know what he's feeling. Disappointment radiates off him like a pulse. For the first time since I've known him, a sort of rift has formed between us. And for all his quiet strength, for all the years I've trusted him to stand by my side, right now he feels distant, like I've taken something precious from him.

I open my mouth to say something, anything, but I can't find the words. I want to tell him that this is the only way, that I didn't abandon Caelan's plans or the rebel army lightly, but the look on Akin's face stops me short. He doesn't look angry. He looks hurt. And I know that hurt isn't just about me choosing another path. It's about the faith he's had in me, the loyalty he's given so freely, now cracked by my decision to chase what he sees as a dangerous myth.

River, on the other hand, has the audacity to look satisfied, a smug smile tugging at the corner of his mouth as he strides beside me. There's an unusual spring in his step that I haven't seen since our journey began, and I'm already feeling wary of it. Whatever is going through his head is not going to be a solution for the rising tensions between us all.

"I just want it noted, for the record, that I didn't trust Caelan from the beginning. I always knew Bright Waters was real, even when you all doubted," he explains, crossing his arms with a casual arrogance that makes my teeth clench. "Guess it turns out I was right, huh?"

I shoot him a glare, but he doesn't flinch, only shrugs with a lopsided grin. "Maybe if you'd listened to me, we wouldn't have wasted so much time with the rebels."

"You're not helping, River," I snap, unable to keep the frustration from my voice. "This isn't about who's right or wrong. It's about doing whatever we have to do to save Altinna, to save my mother. Besides, the fact that you didn't have the balls to speak up like Brook did doesn't make this any better on your part."

River's smile fades a fraction, though he doesn't back down. "I'm just saying it's nice to be proven right once in a while. My only interest in saving your kingdom and your mother is, unfortunately, because you and I are fated. I would've spoken up eventually, when the time was right."

"Whatever. What a shame it is that we are fated," I quip, my anger growing beneath me. "Akin I understood, of course. Brook was a natural choice, as well. I can even make a case for Permiton. But why, oh why, did the fates decide that you needed to be in the mix?"

"You know what, Princess?" River barks, suddenly feeling the need to unleash all of his frustration from the last several days. "I've been nothing but loyal to you since this all started, and not once have you even thrown me a kind word. Hell, Brook even got a pity shag yesterday, but you won't even look at me like I'm worthy of your precious time."

Before I can respond, Brook's quiet voice breaks through the tension. "Arguing isn't going to help anything, and it's definitely not going to get us any closer to Bright Waters."

He's right, of course. The bickering feels petty, pointless. I take a breath, looking away from River's heated expression and focusing instead on the path ahead. Brook falls into step beside me, his presence a comforting contrast to the discord rippling through the group. His newfound confidence is continuing to grow, but it lacks the arrogance of his brother's. For the first time, I feel that he's truly with me on this path, not just following along in silence.

But no matter the confidence, no matter the fire driving us forward, I can't shake the feeling of dread that gnaws at me with every step. It's been days since I left my mother's side, since I last saw her face or heard her voice. Days since I've had any word from Altinna, any reassurance that she's holding on, that Diereken hasn't found a way to break through. And the fear festers inside me, each hour that passes adding another weight pressing down on my heart, another reminder that I might be too late.

I look up at the distant peak, the path winding ever upward, twisting around rocks and through dense thickets. Bright Waters lies somewhere beyond this wilderness, shrouded in mystery and magic, a place most believe doesn't exist. But I have to believe in it. I have to trust that it's real, that this journey has a purpose, that the stories aren't just stories but a hidden truth that will save us all.

"Maerilee."

Akin's voice brings me back, gentle yet firm. I turn to him, and his expression softens just enough for me to glimpse the man I've always relied on, the protector who's stood by me through everything.

He hesitates, and for a moment, I think he's about to apologize or give some reassurance. But instead, he lets out a frustrated sigh, shaking his head. "I'm sorry to doubt you, but I have to admit that I'm still unsure. Obviously, we needed to get away from the army. That was a good plan. But are we sure that Bright Waters isn't a myth after all?"

The doubt stings, but I force myself to hold his gaze, my voice quiet but steady. "I don't know how much time my mother has left, Akin. I don't even know if she's still alive, but I can't just turn back and hope for the best. Every moment we spend here, I feel like I'm failing her, like I'm failing Altinna. I'd rather believe in a myth than to go home empty-handed without trying."

He meets my eyes, the tension still visible, though there's a flicker of understanding. He might not agree, but at least he's starting to see why this matters to me, why I can't just sit back and wait for something to happen.

I have to make it happen.

"I'm here, Maerilee," he says finally, his voice soft. "I'll follow you, even if I don't understand. I'm with you."

The relief that washes over me is bittersweet, a reminder of the loyalty Akin has always shown me, the quiet strength that has carried me through so many battles. But I know that his faith isn't blind, that he still questions this path, and it makes me wonder how many times I can rely on him before he starts to break.

The rest of the day passes in relative silence, each of us lost in our own thoughts, our own fears. I can feel the weight of River and Akin's doubts pressing down, and it only makes my own resolve feel heavier, harder to carry. Every step we take brings me closer to the unknown, closer to the edge of what I can do, and it terrifies me more than I'm willing to admit.

But as the sun begins to dip below the horizon, casting long shadows across the mountainside, I feel a strange sense of peace settle over me. The darkness feels familiar, comforting, a reminder that no matter how far we have to go, no matter what lies ahead, I'm not alone.

· · ·

BROOK

WE'VE BEEN WALKING FOR HOURS WHEN I FINALLY SEE IT, A FAINT glimmer through the trees, a barely-there shimmer that pulls me forward like a silent invitation. The others must see it, too, because they follow without a word, drawn to the strange light filtering through the thick foliage.

And then, as we step into a clearing, there it stands, a monument, half-buried by time, weathered stone etched with runes and symbols that glow faintly, seeming almost alive.

I feel my heart skip a beat as recognition settles over me. I've heard stories of this place my whole life, and now, here it is in front of us–the entrance to Bright Waters.

"This is it," I say, my voice barely more than a whisper. "This is where it begins."

Maerilee's eyes are wide, her gaze fixed on the monument as if trying to absorb every detail. Akin, too, is silent, his face frozen with awe and reverence as he reaches out to touch the ancient stone. I can see the questions in his eyes, the wonder and the doubt as he runs his fingers over the carvings, each one a piece of a story too old to remember.

But when I look over at River, I see something else. His face is set, serious, his usual smugness replaced with a look of dread, a silent understanding that mirrors my own. We both know that finding this entrance isn't the end of our journey. It's only the beginning. Beyond this, our travels will test the limits of our powers, the dedication we have to one another. Bright Waters doesn't reveal itself to everyone, which is why so many believe it's a myth. We have to prove ourselves worthy.

"We're not through yet," River says, and I nod, sharing a glance that speaks volumes. There's a part of me that wonders if we're ready for what lies ahead, if we're truly prepared to face the dangers and challenges waiting in the depths of Bright Waters. But there's no turning back now.

Maerilee steps forward, breaking the silence. "How do we get in?" Her voice is steady, but I can hear the edge of urgency in it, the raw need to press forward, to find whatever it is we need to save her mother.

I study the runes for a moment, feeling the faint pulse of magic in the air. There's a barrier here, something woven deep into the stone, an ancient magic that requires sacrifice.

"It needs a payment," I say, my voice quiet but sure. "We'll each have to make a small offering. In blood."

Maerilee doesn't hesitate, drawing her dagger and pressing it to her palm. I watch as the blade slices her skin, a thin line of crimson welling up on her hand, and then she places her palm against the stone, letting the blood seep into the ancient carvings. Akin follows suit, then River, and finally, I do the same, feeling the sting of the cut, the warmth of my own blood as I press my palm to the stone.

But nothing happens. The light in the runes dims, flickers, then fades entirely, leaving us standing in silence, the entrance still sealed, the way forward closed off.

"What?" Maerilee's voice trails off, frustration evident in her expression as she withdraws her hand, clenching it into a fist. "Why isn't it working? Is it supposed to do this?"

I can see the strain in her eyes, the desperate hope that's been driving her forward now replaced with a flicker of doubt. She lets out a low curse, kicking at the ground, and for a moment, I feel the weight of our journey pressing down on all of us, a reminder that even here, even at the very doorstep of our goal, the path remains elusive.

We didn't come all this way just to be stopped at the door.

But then, a shadow shifts at the edge of the clearing, and I feel a chill run down my spine. I turn, expecting to see that the army has caught up to us, that we'll again be taken into custody.

The figure standing there isn't from the Oceanean army, though. It is, in fact, the very last creature I would expect to see, though I realize now that was just wishful thinking.

15

GATEWAY TO BRIGHT WATERS

THE JOURNEY TO BRIGHT WATERS IS FAR FROM EASY. EVEN IGNORING the difficulty of the mountainous terrain, the Oceanean army lurks on every edge of my awareness, their patrols crisscrossing the region, and I know that at any given moment I could be captured and taken to my death. The path is treacherous, winding through rugged terrain and dense forest, and I keep myself shrouded in shadows, careful to stay hidden. I've taken every measure possible to avoid detection, slipping off the main path to blend with the undergrowth and navigating around the pockets where I can feel soldiers lingering like predators waiting to pounce.

But I know I'm getting close. The pulse of magic grows stronger with each step, a faint resonance in the ground beneath me, guiding me toward Bright Waters. I feel it more acutely now, like a current running through my veins, thrumming with purpose and calling me forward. My Sight tells me I'm on the right path, that I'm close to the others, and that they, too, are closing in on the entrance to Bright Waters.

Finally, the landscape opens to reveal the ancient monument, a towering stone structure draped in vines, its surface etched with intricate symbols that shimmer faintly, as though they're inviting me, waiting for me. A powerful barrier surrounds it, woven into the very air, and the magic here is potent, alive. But there's something else in the clearing, a shadow that doesn't belong.

I stop in my tracks, allowing the Sight to open before me, showing me a vision of what lies ahead–Oceanean soldiers, hidden around the edges of the monument, lie in wait, either for me or Maerilee and the others. I see their forms flicker in my mind, crouched and silent, their weapons at the ready, their eyes fixed on the path where Maerilee and the others will emerge. They're here to ambush the group, to take them down before they can even make it to the entrance.

I won't let that happen.

Drawing my sword, I step into the clearing, keeping my movements fluid and precise, using the element of surprise. The first soldier doesn't even have a chance to react before my blade meets its mark, a clean, silent strike that leaves him crumpling to the ground. The others hear the soft thud, heads snapping toward me, but by then, I'm already moving, slipping between them like a shadow, striking each one down with swift, practiced precision.

The fight is brief, my actions honed and efficient, my senses heightened with the help of my Sight. I can anticipate their movements at the exact moment they decide to make them, cutting them off at the knees both figuratively and literally. By the time the last soldier falls, the clearing is silent once more, and I wipe my blade clean, returning it to its sheath. The tension lingers in the air, but I know the path is now clear.

The others are safe–for now.

I step back into the shadows, just out of sight as I wait. Soon enough, I see them, their familiar forms emerging from the trees, moving cautiously toward the monument. Maerilee follows behind Brook, her eyes wide, her expression one of awe as she takes in the sight of the ancient stone, the runes carved into its surface. Akin follows close behind, his gaze flickering over the clearing, ever vigilant, his hand resting on the hilt of his sword. River takes up the rear, a look of quiet reverence and a certain amount of fear coloring his expression. He's never looked so humbled.

I watch as they approach the entrance, as they press their hands against the stone, offering their blood to the ancient magic. But the monument remains silent, unyielding, the entrance refusing to open. Frustration blooms on Maerilee's face, her jaw clenched as she pulls her hand back, looking up at the stone with a mixture of anger and despair.

I know then that it's time, that I must now reveal myself and explain.

I step out of the shadows, and their heads snap toward me, eyes widening in shock and recognition. Akin's reaction is immediate. He draws his sword, his stance shifting, ready to defend Maerilee at any cost. River and Brook, too, move instinctively, both assuming battle positions, ready to call upon their water magic if they can use it here.

But Maerilee looks at me, her expression unreadable for a moment, and then she moves, stepping forward before any of the others can react. She crosses the distance between us in a few swift strides, her gaze fixed on me, and I don't know what to expect. Anger? Relief? Maybe a mixture of both.

But before I can brace myself, her hand swings up, and she slaps me.

The impact stings, and I blink, surprised, feeling the sharp burn where her hand met my cheek. I haven't even processed it before she's pulling me into an awkward embrace, her arms wrapping around me, her grip tight and fierce.

It takes me a moment to respond, my body stiff, uncertain. But then I let myself relax, my arms slowly wrapping around her in return, holding her as she clings to me, her head buried against my shoulder. All of her tension begins to ease, and I feel a strange warmth spread through me, a sense of connection that goes beyond words, beyond all the doubts and betrayals.

She pulls back, looking up at me with a mixture of anger and relief, her eyes searching my face as though trying to piece together everything that's happened.

"You have so much explaining to do, Permiton," she says, her voice low, steady, but carrying an edge of steel.

"I know," I reply, meeting her gaze. "I deserve that. And I will explain everything. But first…." I gesture toward the monument. "You need my help to get inside."

Akin lets out a scoff, his sword still raised, his expression untrusting. "And why should we believe you, after everything you've done?"

"Because," I say, holding his gaze, unflinching, "I'm the one you need to open this passageway. And whether you trust me or not, we don't have time to argue. The Oceanean soldiers know where we are. I took care of the ones hiding nearby, but more will come. We need to move."

River raises an eyebrow, exchanging a glance with Brook, who gives a slight nod, their silent conversation conveying their shared agreement. They may not like it, but they know the truth in my words. "We're out of options, and the entrance to Bright Waters won't open until the entire party is unified. It's been waiting for us to reconcile, so you'd better decide fast that you forgive me."

Maerilee steps forward, her eyes locked on mine. "Then let's not waste any more time."

I nod, drawing a dagger from my belt, and with a swift, practiced movement, I reopen the cut on my palm, pressing it against the stone where they've already given their blood sacrifices.

Akin, reluctantly, lowers his sword and stairs at the monument, waiting for something to happen, ready to pounce if nothing does. The stone begins to glow, the runes flaring to life, their light brightening as the barrier slowly dissolves. A doorway forms, dark and foreboding, leading into the depths of the mountain.

Maerilee looks at me, a mixture of emotions flickering across her face. I see gratitude, frustration, maybe even a hint of trust.

"Thank you," she says, her voice barely a whisper, but it carries a weight that I feel deep within me.

I nod, meeting her gaze, knowing that whatever lies ahead, we'll face it together. The past may still haunt us, and the wounds of betrayal may not yet be healed, but at this moment, I feel a strange sense of purpose, a connection that transcends all the doubts and fears.

As we step forward, crossing the threshold into the heart of Bright Waters, I know that we'll need each other to face what's ahead.

* * *

MAERILEE

THE ATMOSPHERE AROUND US IMMEDIATELY CHANGES, BECOMING MORE charged with the hum of magic so strong that it nearly takes my breath away. I survey the others to see if they're having a similar reaction and notice that they're all taking it in stride. Part of me thinks they're in disbelief that we've actually made it. My mind is still reeling, realizing that we are that much closer to saving my mother. I take a deep breath to clear my head and allow myself to adjust to the feeling.

I turn to Permiton, pulling his crumpled note from my pocket. His eyes flick down to it, then back up to my face, and I see a glimmer of understanding in his expression, and maybe a hint of hope.

"I received it," I say quietly, holding his gaze. "I had my doubts, but I trusted you enough to come here."

Permiton's expression softens, a subtle nod passing between us. "Thank you, Maerilee," he says, his voice barely above a whisper. He gestures to the edge of the clearing where a handful of Oceanean soldiers lay dead, their bodies serving as a warning to their commander. I can hardly believe that Permiton is the one who's taken them out. He never struck me as a strong fighter. Then again, he's clearly full of surprises.

"I cleared the way for you," he says, his tone steady, even as I see the faint tension in his posture, as though he's still bracing himself for any lingering distrust. "If you believe anything, believe that I would never let you fall into any real harm."

I let out a breath, feeling a strange mixture of relief and apprehension. The other three are watching us, expressions ranging from curiosity to suspicion, and I can sense the weight of the moment pressing down on us all. But whatever doubts remain, I know we don't have time to linger here, to sort through the tangled web of loyalties and betrayals that have brought us to this point.

"We should go," I say, glancing back at the ancient monument. The entrance looms before us, dark and foreboding, shrouded in mist. I turn to Permiton, nodding for him to proceed.

He steps forward, and a sense of awe and trepidation fills me as I watch him cross the threshold into the dark pathway. I follow behind him, with Brook, River, and finally Akin coming after me. The moment Akin steps through the doorway, it's like the forest closes in on itself. Gone is the clearing we were just in. All that's left is the path to Bright Waters.

The air inside is cool, dense with a fog that swirls around us like a living being, curling and twisting as we move deeper into the passage. It feels as though we're walking into another world, a place suspended between reality and myth, where magic hums in every stone, every breath.

The others follow close behind, their footsteps echoing softly in the silence. River and Brook exchange a glance, a silent communication passing between them, and I feel the weight of their understanding settle over me.

They grew up with stories of Bright Waters, tales of its power, its mysteries, but they know, as I do, that the stories only scratched the surface. Whatever awaits us here is far beyond anything we could have imagined.

As we move further into the haze, my pulse quickens, my senses heightening with each step. The fog grows denser, swallowing up the light, leaving us in a dim, silvery glow that seems to emanate from the stone itself. Shadows flicker at the edges of my vision, strange shapes shifting and moving as though the very walls are alive, watching us. Waiting.

I glance back at the others, a nervous smile flickering across my face. "Stay close," I say, my voice barely a whisper, the sound swallowed up by the fog.

Akin's hand rests on his sword, his posture tense, ever vigilant. "We don't know what lies ahead, so let's stay alert. Bright Waters may be powerful, but it won't make our journey any easier."

River scoffs, his voice laced with a hint of his usual arrogance. "You're not scared, are you, Akin? I thought the mighty warrior would be eager to face whatever this place has in store."

Akin gives him a withering look, but he doesn't take the bait. Instead, he moves closer to me, his gaze softening as he studies my face, as though searching for any sign of fear. "Are you all right, Maerilee?"

I nod, though the anxiety coiling in my stomach tells a different story. "I'm fine," I say, forcing a smile. "Just a little nervous."

He nods, a reassuring warmth in his eyes. "I'm by your side. No matter what."

His words bring a small measure of comfort, and I feel my shoulders relax, if only a little.

"Not to agree with River, but it is kind of nice to be right about this place," I tease, sticking my tongue out at him to ease the tension.

He pulls me into a quick, warm embrace, kissing me on the forehead. But as we continue deeper into the passage, the sense of unease only grows, a prickling at the back of my mind, a feeling that we're walking into something far beyond our understanding.

The fog thickens, swirling around us in dense clouds that obscure our path, and I have to fight the urge to reach out, to touch the stone walls, to ground myself in something solid.

Suddenly, the passage widens, dumping us back out into a wide forest, though it is darker and more foreboding than the one we just left.

"This is where the trials begin," Brook tells us quietly, a sense of dread beginning to settle on all of us.

"Will the soldiers be able to find us here?" I ask, though I'm not sure who I'm speaking to. I don't think anyone truly knows what to expect now that we've crossed the barrier.

"They won't be able to get in," Permiton finally assures me, clearly relying on his Sight to show him the future. "Nor will your new allies. Bright Waters will only open to us because our intentions are pure, so for the time being, we don't need to worry about our enemies."

"Now, it's just the Waters themselves that we need to worry about," Brook announces in a foreboding tone.

16

PRIDE COMES BEFORE THE FALL

Akin

We're all exhausted, physically, mentally, and emotionally, and I can see the strain on everyone's faces. Maerilee looks like she's barely holding herself together, her shoulders tense, her eyes flickering with a mix of anxiety and determination. Brook has a heavy sense of authority on his shoulders, now that he's taken the mantle of being our guide through Bright Waters. Even River seems less smug than usual, though I'm sure he'll find a way to change that soon enough.

I don't care to see how Permiton is feeling. After everything he's put us through, he can fend for himself for all I care. But it's still my job to protect Maerilee, and now that means I have to protect these fools, too.

"We should stop here," I say, my voice cutting through the heavy silence. "Rest, gather our strength before we move on. We don't know what's waiting for us further in, and I don't like the idea of going in half-dead. As long as we're safe from the soldiers, we deserve to rest."

Brook glances at me and nods, his agreement quick and sincere. "You're right, Akin. We've pushed ourselves hard, and the journey ahead won't be any easier. Resting now is the smart move."

His words catch me off guard because there's no hesitation, no argument, just a straightforward acknowledgment that I'm making the right call. I'm not used to this coming from anyone but Maerilee. For a moment, I feel a flicker of appreciation for Brook, a sense that maybe we're not so different after all. Maybe, given time, we could even form some kind of understanding, a friendship built on mutual respect and shared goals.

It's a strange thought, but not an unwelcome one.

River, on the other hand, lets out an exaggerated sigh, his arms crossed as he leans against the cavern wall. "Great. More sitting around. Because that's exactly what we need right now."

I shoot him a glare, but before I can respond, Maerilee speaks up, her voice firm despite her exhaustion. "We're resting, River. Akin's right. We can't afford to push ourselves past the breaking point. We have no idea what lies ahead, and this is the first time in days that we don't need to fear what lies behind us. If you have a problem with that, you're free to sit and stew quietly."

River's mouth opens, but whatever retort he was about to unleash dies on his tongue when he sees the look she gives him. To my surprise, he actually stays silent, though the annoyed scowl on his face makes it clear he's not happy about it.

Permiton stays out of the conversation entirely, watching us all with that infuriatingly calm expression, as if he's somehow above the tension that's been simmering between us. I don't trust him. I don't care what he's done to prove his so-called loyalty or how easily Maerilee has forgiven him. Every time I look at him, all I see is the man who handed us over to the Oceaneans without a second thought.

The fact that Maerilee doesn't see it, or worse, chooses to ignore it, only makes it harder for me to hold my tongue. She's too trusting, too willing to believe in people who have already let her down. I can't let that happen again. I won't let that happen again.

We settle down in the clearing of the forest, spreading out blankets and unpacking what little supplies we have left. The moon is brighter here, and I wonder if it's the same one we've left behind or if somehow we've been transported to another world altogether. Even so, I allow myself to take it in, to appreciate the beauty of this place despite the danger that hangs over us. It's peaceful in a way that feels almost deceptive, as if the calm is only a mask for the trials that lie ahead.

Maerilee chooses to rest beside me, and I can feel the weight of her presence, her utter exhaustion tinged with just the smallest bit of hope. She doesn't say anything, doesn't ask me the questions I know are lingering in her mind, and I'm grateful for it. I don't want to talk. I don't want to tell her about the doubts gnawing at the edges of my thoughts, the fear that I'm not enough to protect her from what's coming.

Instead, I lay quietly, my hand resting on the hilt of my sword, my eyes scanning the shadows that flicker at the edges of the forest. I don't trust this place. I don't trust the magic that hums in the air or the silence that feels too perfect, too still. And I definitely don't trust Permiton, no matter what Maerilee may think.

I turn my head to watch him as he makes his bed far away from the rest of us, his face unreadable and his movements precise. There's something about him that sets my nerves on edge, something I can't quite pin down. He's too calm, too composed, and it makes me wonder what's going on in that mind of his, what secrets he's keeping from us.

Maerilee shifts beside me, her head resting lightly against my shoulder, and I feel a pang of guilt for letting my thoughts stray. She's given me her trust, chosen to rely on me even when I've questioned myself, and I owe it to her to be strong, to be the protector she needs.

I glance down at her, watching the rise and fall of her chest as she breathes, and the way the light from the moon casts a soft glow over her features. She looks so small, so fragile, and yet, I know better than anyone how much strength she carries within her. She's endured so much, faced so many hardships, but she keeps moving forward, driven by a determination that I can only admire.

I don't voice my fears to her. I don't need to. They're mine to carry, my burden to bear, and I've made my choice. No matter what happens, no matter who or what stands in our way, I will protect her. I will take out anyone who threatens her safety, who dares to put her in harm's way, even if it means turning on those who call themselves allies.

Even if it means facing Permiton.

The thought lingers in my mind as I settle against the soft earth of the forest floor, my grip tightening on my sword. I don't know what lies ahead, what dangers we'll face in the depths of Bright Waters, but I do know one thing. I won't let anything happen to Maerilee, not while I'm still breathing.

Brook's voice breaks the silence, soft and steady.

"It's going to be a long journey," he says, his voice far away. "Even compared to what we've faced already, there are dangers still to come."

I glance at him, surprised by the warning in his voice. It's foreboding, almost like his words are coming from the Waters themselves, and not from him.

River, of course, mutters something under his breath, his usual arrogance slipping back into place as he stretches out on his blanket. I ignore him, focusing instead on the quiet, steady rhythm of Maerilee's breathing.

As the others settle in for the night, I keep my eyes on the shadows, my senses alert. The Bright Waters may hold the answers we're searching for, but I know better than to let my guard down. Danger is always waiting, always lurking just out of sight.

And I'll be ready for it. For her. Always.

* * *

MAERILEE

. . .

THE FIRST RAYS OF SUNLIGHT FILTER THROUGH THE TREES, CASTING A soft glow over the group as we stir from sleep. It shimmers through the dense fog, creating patterns in the darkness. It should be beautiful, comforting even, but I can't shake the knot of anxiety twisting in my stomach. Every step we've taken to get here has been riddled with danger and doubt, and I know the worst is yet to come.

Brook and River are the first to rise, their movements contrasting in a way that's become all too familiar. Brook moves quietly, unassumingly, as he begins to gather the small rations of food we have left and makes a humble breakfast. River stretches dramatically, yawning as if to remind us all that he's here and expects attention. His usual smirk is firmly in place, and I can tell he's gearing up to take charge.

"We need to get moving soon," River declares, running a hand through his hair and glancing around the group as if daring anyone to argue. "The sooner we push through, the sooner we find what we're looking for."

Brook raises an eyebrow but says nothing, his expression calm as he begins doling out servings of our breakfast into small, metal bowls he must have nicked from the rebels. It's clear he doesn't intend to challenge River outright, but there's a quiet confidence in the way he readies himself, as though he already knows this landscape better than any of us.

The rest of us slowly rise, stretching our tired limbs and mentally preparing ourselves for what lies ahead. We eat our breakfast in silence, knowing that we might not have a chance to stop again for a while.

Once we've packed up and begun our journey, the terrain ahead becomes clearer. Jagged cliffs rise in the distance, their edges sharp and unforgiving, while the path winds precariously along steep drops and dense thickets. The air is cool and heavy, carrying the faint scent of damp earth and something metallic, almost magical, that I can't quite place.

River strides ahead, his posture radiating authority, but it quickly becomes apparent that his confidence far outweighs his knowledge. He pauses frequently, glancing around as if trying to orient himself, and the more I watch him, the more it becomes clear; he has no idea where he's going.

"Keep up," he says over his shoulder, his tone impatient as he gestures vaguely toward the rocky path ahead. "This way."

Brook exchanges a glance with me, and I catch the flicker of doubt in his eyes. I can tell he knows this terrain better, that he's more attuned to the subtle shifts in the landscape, the signs that guide us. But he doesn't say anything, instead following quietly as River leads us further along the trail.

It isn't until we reach a narrow ridge that things come to a head. River strides forward confidently, gesturing for us to follow, but something about the path ahead makes my heart stop. The ground slopes downward sharply, the edges crumbling into what looks like an endless drop. The trail is barely wide enough for one person, and as River takes another step, the loose stones beneath his feet give way, sending a cascade of gravel tumbling into the void below.

"River, stop!" I shout, my voice cutting through the morning air.

He freezes, turning to glance back at me with an annoyed expression. "What? I've got it under control."

"You're about to walk us off a cliff!" I snap, gesturing to the precarious edge just inches from his boots.

River looks down, his smirk faltering as he realizes the danger. He takes a careful step back, his confidence visibly shaken, but his pride won't let him admit it. "Fine," he mutters. "We'll go a different way."

"Brook," I say, turning to him, "you're leading from now on."

Brook shrugs, as if he's expected this and was just waiting for someone to say it out loud.

River bristles at my words, his face flushing with anger. "I know exactly what I'm doing," he protests, his voice rising. "This isn't—"

"This isn't about your ego. It's about getting us to Bright Waters safely. River. Brook and Permiton know more about this place than you ever will. Your brother has gotten us this far, so he's in charge of guiding us from now on." My tone is sharp, and he doesn't argue further.

Permiton steps forward, his expression calm but resolute. "Maerilee's right. The terrain here is treacherous, and navigating it requires more than guesswork."

River glares at him, his fists clenching at his sides, but he doesn't speak. Instead, he stalks back to the group, muttering under his breath. His mood is unmistakable, brooding and bitter, his pride wounded in a way that I know will take time to heal.

Brook steps forward hesitantly, glancing at me as if seeking reassurance. I nod, giving him a small smile. "Lead the way, Brook. We trust you."

His posture straightens slightly, a flicker of confidence returning to his expression as he takes the lead. The group falls into step behind him, and I can't help but feel a sense of relief as he guides us along a safer, steadier path. He moves with purpose, his eyes scanning the terrain, reading the subtle cues that I wouldn't have noticed, the way the rocks shift underfoot, the faint markings in the earth that indicate a trail.

As we move higher into the mountains, the landscape grows more challenging, the air thinner and colder. The silence between us is heavy, broken only by the occasional rustle of leaves or the distant call of a bird. River keeps to himself, his face set in a scowl, while Akin remains watchful, his gaze flicking between the group and the surrounding forest.

Permiton walks beside me, his presence steady but quiet. I glance at him, my thoughts lingering on the way he's managed to regain some of our trust, even after everything. It's a tentative truce, one that still feels fragile, but for now, it's enough.

Brook pauses at a fork in the path, studying the ground before choosing the left trail. "This way," he says, his voice calm but certain.

I follow without hesitation, my faith in him growing with each step. There's a quiet strength in the way he leads, a confidence that feels earned rather than assumed. It's a stark contrast to River's bluster, and I find myself appreciating the balance Brook brings to the group.

The sun climbs higher in the sky, casting long shadows over the rocky terrain, but I remind myself that this journey is worth the difficulties. We're not just walking toward Bright Waters; we're walking toward answers, toward the chance to save Altinna and my mother.

And as I glance around at the group, at the faces of the men who have become so dear to me, I feel a flicker of something I haven't felt in a long time.

Hope.

17

RENEWED FAITH

Maerilee

THE SUN BEATS DOWN ON US MERCILESSLY AS WE TRUDGE FORWARD, THE rocky terrain stretching endlessly in every direction. My legs ache, and every step feels heavier than the last, but I push on. We have to. There's no room for weakness now, not with the stakes as high as they are.

Brook leads the way with Akin and River close behind, their sharp gazes scanning the horizon for any sign of danger. I follow, and Permiton lingers at the rear, as silent and enigmatic as ever.

The landscape changes as we go. The jagged hills grow steeper, the vegetation sparser. By the time we reach the base of a tall cliff, the sun is sinking low in the sky, casting long shadows across the ground. The cliff towers over us, a wall of stone that seems almost impossible to scale. My heart sinks at the sight of it. There doesn't seem to be a path around it.

Brook turns to face us, his usually lighthearted expression somber.

"This is it," he says, his voice quiet but firm. "The Bright Waters are at the top of this cliff. But it won't be as simple as climbing it. Once we're up there, the real challenge begins."

"The real challenge?" Akin's voice is tense, his brows furrowed. "What does that mean?"

Brook hesitates, glancing at each of us before answering. "There are trials, magical ones. The Bright Waters don't let just anyone approach. They test you. Each of us will face something different, and it won't be easy."

The words hang in the air like a storm cloud. Akin's jaw tightens, and I can see the unease flickering in his eyes. Even River, usually so cocky and composed, looks troubled. Permiton's expression remains unreadable, though his golden eyes seem to darken slightly.

"Magical trials," Akin mutters, his voice almost a whisper. "Fantastic. Never mind that some of us don't have magic."

I step closer to him, reaching out to take his hand. His fingers are cold, stiff, but I hold on tightly. "We'll get through this," I say softly, meeting his gaze. "Together."

He looks at me for a long moment before nodding, though the tension doesn't leave his face. "Together," he echoes, but his tone lacks conviction.

Brook clears his throat. "I assume the cliff is a trial for you, Akin," he says carefully, so as to not upset him. "It will test your strength and your ability to guide the rest of us. But we shouldn't attempt the climb now. It's too dangerous in the dark. I think we should set up camp here and start at first light."

"I agree," Akin declares, surprising me.

It seems that he and Brook are getting closer, which is a bonus for all of us. If we're all meant to spend the rest of our lives together, it would be helpful for my Four to get along with each other, though I'm not sure River will ever be built for playing nice.

For his part, though, he doesn't question Brook's authority or try to argue. After our journey so far, we're all too exhausted to protest, and the thought of tackling the cliff after a night of rest is far more appealing than attempting it now, though only just slightly.

We build a fire and go through our rations, scraping together a

decent meal. It's a good thing we still had food left as there's no vegetation up here to rely on. River is able to conjure some water for us to
drink deeply and rehydrate. So far, it's the most helpful thing he's
done on this entire journey.

The fire crackles softly as night falls, its warm glow a stark
contrast to the cold bite of the evening air. River sharpens his blade
with a methodical rhythm, the sound of metal on stone filling the
silence. Brook sits nearby, sketching something into the dirt with a
stick, his brow furrowed in concentration. Akin sits next to him, and
they chat together, strategizing about the plan for tomorrow.
Permiton stands just beyond the circle of firelight, leaning against a
tree with his arms crossed, his face a mask of shadow and flickering
gold.

I watch him for a moment, the weight of unspoken words pressing
heavily on my chest. I've avoided this conversation for too long, and I
know I can't put it off any longer. Taking a deep breath, I rise,
brushing the dirt from my skirt. The others glance at me as I move,
their expressions curious but not questioning. I ignore them and
make my way toward Permiton.

He doesn't move as I approach, his gaze fixed on some distant
point in the darkness. "Do you have a moment?" I ask quietly, my
voice steady despite the storm of emotions swirling inside me.

He tilts his head slightly, his golden eyes catching the firelight as
he looks at me. For a moment, he says nothing, and I wonder if he'll
refuse. But then he nods and pushes away from the tree, gesturing for
me to follow him. We find a nearby cave mouth, away from the
others. It's darker here, with only the light of the moon to guide us,
but Permiton's steps are sure as if he can see in the darkness. For all I
know, he can.

He gently takes my hand, guiding me inside and onto a large slab
of rock that makes an excellent bench. I lower myself onto it, and he
sits across from me, his posture relaxed but his gaze sharp.

"We should probably discuss what happened," I begin, my tone
firm. "If I'm going to keep trusting you, I need to know some things,

specifically why you…." I trail off, the words catching in my throat–betrayed us, betrayed me.

He raises an eyebrow, his expression unreadable. "What do you want to know?"

"Everything," I say, the word coming out more forcefully than I intended. "But let's start with why you sold us out to the Oceanean army."

His gaze drops to the ground, and for a moment, I think he won't answer. But then he sighs and looks back at me, his eyes filled with something I can't quite place. Regret? Pain? Something deeper?

"You think I wanted to do that to you?" he says quietly, his voice laced with bitterness. "You think I enjoyed being the villain in your story?"

"You tell me," I reply, my voice sharp. "All I know is that you made a choice, a choice that put all of us in danger."

His jaw tightens, and he makes a noise that sounds an awful lot like a scoff. "You have no idea the vile things those soldiers would have done to you if I hadn't intervened. If we'd tried to fight, it would have ended in a bloodbath."

"You could have told me," I counter. "While we were waiting on that shore, you could have told me about your visions and trusted me to handle what needed to be done. I spent days hating you, believing that you were a traitor, thinking that you'd betrayed us from the very moment you came to Altinna."

"It isn't up to me to change your feelings," he says simply, his voice detached. "I can only tell you the truth and hope you believe me, but I can't make you change your mind."

I blink, taken aback, offended by his coldness. "I've already decided to forgive you," I tell him earnestly. "But why should I continue to trust you when you've given me no reason to? You keep everything so close to your chest, but this partnership is not going to work if you're not honest with me. I don't even care if the others don't trust you, but you are fated to be with me, and you owe it to me to build trust between us."

He leans forward and sighs heavily, his demeanor starting to crack. "I was afraid that if I told you what I saw, you wouldn't be able to stomach what would happen next. They would have slaughtered the four of us, Maerilee, but they weren't going to kill you. Not until they broke you completely, and even then they would have probably kept torturing you just for the fun of it."

My breath catches in my throat as the clarity of his words washes over me, a sick, cold feeling forming in my gut. I nearly collapse from the weight of his words, but he catches me, holding me close as he strokes my hair.

"This is why I couldn't tell you," he whispers gently into my ear. "I didn't want you to live with the dread. I would never have let them hurt you, and pretending to be against you was our best shot at making it out of there alive."

I stare at him, my mind racing to process his words. "So betraying us was the only way that you could protect us?"

"Yes," he says simply. "I'll do whatever it takes to keep you safe, Maerilee. Even if it means you'll hate me for it."

The weight of his words sinks in, pressing against my chest. For so long, I've viewed him as a betrayer, a liar, a threat. But now I see something else, the truth of who he is. I see him as a man willing to sacrifice his own honor, his own place among us, to ensure the survival of all of us.

"You're infuriating," I mutter, my voice shaking with suppressed emotion.

A ghost of a smile flickers across his lips. "So I've been told."

I can't help but laugh at this as I lean up to kiss him. Unlike our first time together, there's no awkwardness to him now. He isn't as stiff, and I realize that it's because the last time he was fulfilling an obligation. Now, he actually cares about me. He proved that when he saved our lives.

Fueled by that knowledge, I climb onto his lap, straddling him as I cradle his face in my hands. Permiton is a lot of things. He's mysterious, he's a loner, he takes on the burden of knowledge by himself because he seems untrustworthy. But he's also a man, and one who's never been properly appreciated. I can tell it in his hesitancy, in his shyness.

His hands rest on my backside gently, as I press myself against him, already feeling his hardness underneath me. I move off him for just a moment, wanting to be as bare in front of him as he was with me. I want him to understand how deeply I trust him, that I am willing to give him everything.

I slip off my clothing quickly, my pale skin glowing in what little moonlight manages to find us in the cavern. I hear his breath catch in his throat and I know he wants this. I climb back on top of him, stripping him of his shirt as I kiss down his neck, run my fingers along his bare chest. He trembles beneath my touch, his breath already coming in short, labored pants.

"I didn't know it could be like this," he hisses, though I don't think he meant for me to hear. I giggle slightly as I grab his hands, moving them to my breasts, giving him permission to touch me there, to explore my body.

He's a quick learner, replacing one hand with his tongue, moving me so that I'm lying on top of our clothes on the stone bench, protected from the cool of the elements. It's a thoughtful gesture, one I realize I didn't think him capable of.

He takes his time, his careful touches becoming rougher, more sure as he explores every inch of me. He teases, touches, bites, sucks, methodically finds every part of me that can possibly feel good, even places I don't expect. He's like a young musician learning an instrument for the first time. He's eager to press all of the right notes.

But I soon can't take anymore, my body so tightly coiled from the pleasure he's building. I need release, and I need to feel him on top of me, inside of me, all over me.

"Permiton," I whisper shakily. "Please."

He looks at me with a surprised expression, as if he forgot that this is an act meant for two. He's spent what feels like hours lavishing my body with his praise. It's my turn.

I squeeze his shoulder, directing him back up to me, capturing his lips with mine as I reach down to tug down his pants and find his hard, large member. I stroke it gently once, then twice, feeling his excitement trickle out.

He gazes at me carefully, unsure, but I nod, guiding him to my entrance. He makes love to me–there's no other way to describe it. He is gentle, yet effusive with his ravishment. He brings me to the peak of my pleasure so quickly, I have to hold onto him for dear life.

He's right behind, his body convulsing with the force of his release.

He collapses next to me, pulling me against him to keep me warm.

18

A STEEP CLIMB

Akin

I WAIT FOR MAERILEE, BUT SHE DOESN'T COME BACK THAT NIGHT. IT turns my stomach, nearly sends me into a rage when I realize that she's spending the night with Permiton. What does she possibly see in him? What smooth words can he possibly offer her to explain away his indiscretions? It's not that she's with another man. I've gotten used to it. It's that she's with him!

He's a traitor, pure and simple. I don't care what she believes. This is one point I can't trust her on. I've followed her here, and I've seen that she is often right, but for some reason, Permiton is a blind spot for her.

I eventually slip into a fitful, restless sleep, often hoping I'll wake up, and she'll be beside me, but when I awake in the morning, she and Permiton are walking back to our camp, looking freshly fucked and bright as the sun.

Part of me wonders what would happen to Maerilee's powers if Permiton were to "accidentally" fall off the cliff to his death. It's a selfish thought, of course. She clearly cares for him, and she needs him to strengthen her powers. It doesn't mean I'm happy about it. It may tactically be advantageous to trust him, to form an alliance with him the way I've done with Brook, but it will be a cold day in hell before that ever happens.

When we're finally ready to start the journey, we stand in a line, staring up at the face of the cliff. The rock face stretches upward, jagged and unyielding, its steep incline mocking us. I can see the others looking at the sheer cliff with varying degrees of apprehension, except Brook, who spent the better part of last night strategizing this climb with my input. For me, this climb is just another challenge, one I know I'm physically capable of conquering. I've trained my entire life for tasks like this, my body conditioned to endure, my mind sharp enough to calculate each move.

But this isn't just about what I'm physically capable of. This is also a test of my leadership, of my ability to get my companions safely through this challenge. They aren't warriors. They don't have years of combat training or the instincts to navigate terrain like this.

And that terrifies me.

Damn, now would be a good time to have use of our wings.

The first few feet are simple enough for all of us. I move quickly, testing the holds as I climb, scanning the path ahead for the best route. The wind whips against the cliff face, cool and sharp, and I can feel the elements pressing against us, relentless in their indifference.

"Put your hand here," I call down to Maerilee, pointing to a solid grip. "And your foot there, on that ledge."

She nods, her expression focused, but I can see the strain in her arms and legs as she reaches for the holds. Behind her, Brook is making steady progress, his movements slower but deliberate. River, on the other hand, curses loudly every few minutes, his frustration clear as he struggles to find purchase on the stone. The prince is, no doubt, unused to such hard work.

"Why don't we just grow our wings and fly up?" he mutters, his tone dripping with sarcasm. "Wouldn't that be easier?"

"Because none of us are feathered fae, and complaining isn't going to get us to the top," I snap back, the edge in my voice sharper than I intended. I can't afford distractions right now, not with Maerilee climbing just below me. Every instinct in my body is screaming at me to keep her safe, but how can I protect her when my hands are gripping this rock?

"We would be if we did a binding," River calls. "Let's all just climb down and do the binding ceremony together so we can get our wings. That would make this much easier."

"The Waters would reject it, you idiot," Brook snaps in anger. "The point of these tests is to challenge us. The cliff is Akin's challenge."

"You're kidding me!" River screams back. "Are you telling me that if the magicless fae were not here, there would be no cliff? Maerilee, are you sure he's one of us?"

"Shut up, you dolt," she shoots back. "I need to concentrate. We all do."

Satisfied with her retort and not feeling the need to give River a piece of my mind, I guide the group higher.

The climb becomes steeper, the holds smaller and more precarious. I pause every few minutes to call down instructions, guiding them as best I can, but it's slow going. The higher we climb, the more exposed we are, the wind growing fiercer, the drop below us a constant reminder of the stakes.

I glance down to check on Maerilee, my heart clenching at the sight of her struggling to reach the next hold. Her hands are trembling, her knuckles white as she clings to the rock, but she doesn't complain. She's stronger than she gives herself credit for, and that strength only makes me more determined to see her safely to the top.

"Just a little further," I call, trying to keep my voice steady, reassuring. "You're doing great."

She doesn't respond, but I can see the flicker of determination in her eyes, the way her jaw tightens as she forces herself to keep going. I move ahead and am testing the next section of the climb when I hear it—a deadly scream that chills me to my core.

"Maerilee!" I shout, my voice raw with panic. I look down just in time to see her foot slip off a ledge, her body jerking as she loses her balance. She's dangling now, her hands gripping the rock with desperate strength, her legs flailing as she searches for a foothold.

"Hold on!" I yell, my heart pounding in my chest. My muscles tense as I instinctively start to climb back down, but the angle is too steep, the distance between us too far. I'm helpless, forced to watch as she struggles, and the realization hits me like a blow. I can't reach her in time.

"No!" I scream, my voice hoarse, as I see her grip falter. Her fingers slip from the rock, and for a moment, time seems to freeze. She's falling, her body tumbling toward the jagged rocks below, and I can't do anything to stop it.

But then, out of nowhere, Permiton reacts. He's below her, his movements swift and precise, and in an instant, he reaches out and grabs her wrist, stopping her fall. The force of the catch jerks them both downward, but Permiton braces himself against the cliff, his other hand gripping a secure hold.

"Find your footing!" he shouts, his voice calm but commanding. "Now!"

Maerilee scrambles, her legs kicking against the rock until she finds a small ledge to rest on. Permiton steadies her, his hand still wrapped around her wrist, his face a mask of focus.

"Are you all right?" I hear him ask, his voice softer now, his gaze searching her face.

She nods shakily, her breathing ragged. "I think so. Thank you."

I stare down at them, my chest heaving with a mixture of relief and lingering fear. I want to be angry, to yell at her for scaring me like that, but all I can feel is gratitude that she's safe, that Permiton, of all people, was there to catch her.

The rest of the climb is a blur, every muscle in my body aching with tension as I force myself to focus on getting to the top. By the time I finally pull myself over the edge and onto solid ground, my arms are trembling, my breath coming in ragged gasps. The others follow one by one, their movements slow and exhausted, until we're all lying on the grass at the top of the cliff, staring up at the sky.

I sit up quickly, my eyes scanning the group until they land on

Maerilee. She's sitting cross-legged a few feet away, her face pale but relieved, her arms wrapped around herself as she catches her breath. I move to her side without thinking, kneeling in front of her and gripping her shoulders gently.

"Are you hurt?" I ask, my voice low, urgent. "Let me see."

She gives me a small, reassuring smile, though her hands are still trembling. "I'm fine, Akin. Just a few scrapes and bruises. Nothing serious."

My eyes flick over her, searching for any sign of injury, and I notice the shallow scratches on her arms, the dirt smudging her skin. It's not as bad as I feared, but the memory of her falling, the helplessness I felt watching it happen, still lingers like a phantom pain. I pull her against me in a careful, but firm, embrace.

"I thought I lost you," I admit, my voice barely above a whisper.

Her expression softens, and she reaches out, resting a hand on my face. "You didn't. And you won't."

She kisses me gently, reassuring me that she's okay, that we're going to be okay. It does little to allay the anxiety in my chest, but I cling to her like a lifeline. It's been a long day, my limbs have nearly given out, so I can't even imagine how much more difficult it was for the rest of them. But I can't let go of Maerilee. I don't ever want her out of my embrace again.

I glance over at Permiton, who's standing a short distance away, his expression unreadable as he watches us. My jaw tightens, the words catching in my throat, but I force myself to say them.

"Thank you," I say hoarsely as I hold her against my chest. "For saving her."

Permiton meets my gaze, his silver-gray eyes steady. "I would never let anything happen to her," he says simply. "If you believe anything at all, believe that."

I want to believe him, but the lingering doubts in my mind make it hard to trust. Still, at this moment, I can't deny the truth of what he's done. He caught her when I couldn't. He saved her life. And for that, I owe him something, even if it's only the barest acknowledgment of his actions.

Maerilee squeezes my arm gently, drawing my attention back to her.

"We're all here," she says softly. "We made it—because of you. That's what matters."

I nod, the tension in my chest easing just enough for me to breathe again. She's right. We're here, together, and that's what matters. But as I look out at the landscape stretching before us, at the distant shimmer of the Bright Waters in the horizon, I can't shake the feeling that this climb was only the beginning.

I'm not equipped to get us through the next part, and it kills me.

19

SWEET NOTHINGS

The air at the top of the cliff is cooler, sharper, and the electric hum of magic is only getting stronger the closer we get to the Waters. My body aches from the climb, but standing here, looking out over the rugged, unforgiving terrain below and the shimmering haze ahead that marks Bright Waters, I feel an intense rush of dopamine. We've made it this far, and we'll make it the rest of the way too. I also begin to understand that we're only going to make it together. For the first time in my life, I feel like I'm exactly where I'm supposed to be.

The rest of the group takes a moment to catch their breath, their exhaustion palpable. Maerilee has nearly collapsed against Akin, who has her in a tight grip. After her fall, he's completely unwilling to leave her side, though he isn't the only one who feared for her. Still, I know that he needs this more than I do right now, so I don't let it bother me.

River leans against a rock, muttering something about how this journey could have been easier without the "magicless bodyguard." I only roll my eyes and ignore him, annoyed by his continued arrogance. Part of me thinks he still hasn't fully accepted that Maerilee doesn't belong to only him. He isn't used to sharing. He's never had to before, least of all with me. Not having his way is really taking a toll on him, and I'm somewhat disappointed that he hasn't grown from this experience at all.

My gaze shifts to Permiton, who is studying the path ahead, his eyes narrowed in concentration. The ground between us and Bright Waters is literally unclear. A faint shimmer hangs in the air, marking a series of magical traps designed to keep out anyone unworthy of the Waters. I used to read extensively about these traps, safe in my castle and secure in the knowledge that I would likely never have to take them on myself.

Now that we're here, my dread is starting to grow exponentially as I recall all that I learned when I was just a lonely, bored child reading about theoretical dangers.

"We're not getting through that without disarming these traps," Permiton says, his tone matter-of-fact as he gestures to the shimmering barrier. "The magic is old, but it's layered. We'll need to be careful."

I step forward, surprising even myself.

"I can help," I tell him, my voice steadier than I expected.

Permiton turns to me, his expression unreadable for a moment before he nods. "Good. We'll need all the magic we can muster."

For a moment, I feel the weight of the others' eyes on me, curious, uncertain, but I push past the self-doubt that tries to creep in. This is my chance to prove myself, to contribute something meaningful to this mission. I've spent so much of my life in the background, overlooked and underestimated, but here, now, I have a role to play.

I know more about these traps than anyone, Permiton included, and I have the advantage of being on home turf. My magic is fueled by the same enchantment that powers Bright Waters. I can do this.

Permiton and I move closer to the traps, the protective magic humming in the air around us like an unseen current. I can feel it pulsing beneath my skin, a strange, intoxicating sensation that sets my nerves alight. He begins tracing symbols in the air, his movements precise and deliberate, and I follow his lead, letting my own magic flow through me as I weave it into the pattern.

The first trap is a simple barrier spell, designed to repel intruders with brute force. I focus on unraveling the threads of the spell, pulling them apart one by one, while Permiton stabilizes the magic to prevent it from collapsing on us. It's delicate work, requiring focus and precision, but as we move through it, I feel something shift within me.

My confidence grows with each successful step, the flow of my magic becoming stronger, more natural. I've always been hesitant, afraid of drawing attention to myself or making a mistake, but now there's no room for hesitation. The group is counting on me, and for the first time, I feel like I'm truly part of something bigger than myself.

The next trap is more complex, a shifting maze of light and shadow that moves to confuse and disorient anyone who steps into it. Permiton glances at me, a small smirk tugging at the corner of his mouth.

"Do you think you're up for this?"

I nod, a spark of determination flaring within me. "I can handle it," I assure him as we step forward in unison.

Together, we dive into the maze, our magic intertwining as we work to put the shadows and light in their proper places. The light shifts around us, flickering and twisting in ways that make my head spin, but I force myself to focus, to see beyond the illusions. My water magic flows through me, steady and strong, carving a path through the shifting shadows and clearing the way for the others to follow.

As we move through the traps, I can feel my powers growing stronger, more refined. It's as if a dam has broken within me, releasing a flood of energy I didn't know I had. And I know why. It's Maerilee. She's the reason for all of this, the reason I've pushed myself beyond my limits, the reason I've found the strength to stand on my own. Without her, I wouldn't have access to such strong magic, but more importantly, I wouldn't have such faith in myself.

I glance back at her, watching as she follows behind us, her silver hair catching the faint light of the traps. She's watching me, her expression unreadable, but there's something in her gaze that makes my chest tighten. It's not just admiration or gratitude. It's something deeper, something I want to believe might be reflected in my own eyes.

When we finally reach the last trap, a complex puzzle of runes etched into the ground, Permiton and I pause, our breathing heavy but triumphant. "You're good at this," he says, his tone almost teasing. "You've impressed me far beyond what I expected."

I manage a small smile, the compliment catching me off guard. "Thanks, I think," I manage.

With the final trap disarmed, the path ahead clears, the shimmer of magic dissipating to reveal the entrance to Bright Waters. The air is heavy with anticipation, and I can feel the tension in the group ease slightly as we realize we've made it through another trial.

Akin finally releases Maerilee as he steps toward the Waters on his own, his sword drawn as he assesses the risks. He's not going to let Maerilee anywhere near the place if it poses any threat to her. I use his distraction to my advantage.

As the others prepare to move forward, I step away from the group, my heart pounding as I make my way to her. She looks up at me, her silver eyes bright with curiosity and something else I can't quite name.

"Maerilee," I begin, my voice soft but steady, "can I talk to you for a moment?"

She nods, stepping away from the others to join me. "Of course. What's on your mind?"

I hesitate, the words catching in my throat, but then I remind myself of everything we've been through, everything she's inspired in me.

"I just," I start, trying to find the words. "I wanted to thank you," I say, my words tumbling out in a rush, "for believing in me, for giving me a chance to prove myself. I've spent so much of my life feeling like I don't matter, like I'm just a shadow in the background. But with you, I feel different. I feel like I'm part of something important."

Her expression softens, her gaze steady and reassuring. "You are important, Brook. You've always been important to me. I'm glad you see that now."

Her words fill me with a warmth I've never known, and before I can second-guess myself, I take a step closer, my heart pounding.

"I love you, Maerilee," I say, my voice barely above a whisper. "I don't know when it happened, or how, but I do. I love you."

For a moment, she's silent, her eyes searching mine, and I feel my heart stutter in my chest. But then she smiles, a soft, radiant smile that takes my breath away, and she steps closer, her hand brushing against mine.

"I think I've known that," she says, her voice just as soft. "And I think I love you too, Brook."

Before I can respond, she leans in, her lips brushing against mine in a kiss that sends a jolt of electricity through me. It's soft at first, tentative, but then it deepens, the warmth between us growing as I wrap my arms around her, holding her close.

For the first time, I feel truly alive, truly whole.

When we finally pull apart, I catch a flicker of movement out of the corner of my eye. I glance over to see River watching us, his jaw tight, his expression unreadable. A pang of guilt twists in my chest, but I push it aside. This moment is ours, and nothing, not even River's jealousy, can take it away.

Maerilee smiles up at me, her hand resting lightly on my chest. "We should catch up with the others," she says, her voice soft but steady.

I nod, taking her hand in mine as we turn to rejoin the group. Whatever lies ahead, I know we'll face it together. And for the first time in my life, I'm looking forward to the future.

2 0

REALITY CHECK

The path winds endlessly through the rocky terrain, the air thick with the hum of magic. I should feel some sense of triumph, I suppose. After all, we're nearing Bright Waters, the mythical source of all of the power in Oceana. Legend has it that it is the single greatest source of power in the entire realm, maybe in all of the realms. But all I feel is frustration, a simmering anger that burns low and constant, its flames licking at the edges of my thoughts.

For days now, I've watched Maerilee grow closer to everyone but me. Akin is always at her side, a steady rock she leans on without hesitation. He, at least, I can understand. He has been her bodyguard for so many years. There's been a trust there that runs deeper than Bright Waters themselves. Even if I don't exactly like Akin, I can respect their bond.

But how the hell has she allowed Permiton to worm his way back into her good graces? None of us missed the way they ran off together last night and didn't return to our camp until the early daylight hours. Now that he's rescued her from her fall, even Akin has

127

seemed to forgive him for what he did. I'll never forgive, though, and I'll never forget. One of us has to stay grounded enough to remember how he betrayed us.

Even Brook, my quiet, brooding brother, has found a way to matter to her. I heard their sickening expressions of love to one another. Leave it to Brook to be so sappy about this all. He had to go and fall in love with her.

Which leaves me out in the cold. I'm the outsider, the one she barely tolerates, the one she snaps at every time I open my mouth. She hates me, and for no good reason. I've been on this journey enduring just as much as everyone else. Yet, I'm left out of every decision, every strategy meeting. Maerilee doesn't even speak to me. She just assumes I'm going to follow along like a loyal puppy.

If it weren't for Brook telling me about Permiton's note, I wouldn't have even been included in the plan to leave the rebels. Would she have just left me there to get taken or murdered by the Oceanean army? Part of me believes she would have. She clearly doesn't give a damn whether I live or die, so long as she still gets access to my power.

It wasn't always like this. Before I met Maerilee, I was the Crown Prince of Oceana. People listened when I spoke. They laughed at my jokes, hung on my every word. My charm was my weapon, my title my shield. But here, all of that is gone. I'm not a prince anymore. I'm just River, a son of nowhere, with no land, no title, and no idea what the future holds. Somehow I've become less worthy and desirable than my miserable brother.

The worst part is watching her look at everyone else the way I wish she'd look at me. There's something about Maerilee–her fire, her determination, the way she carries the weight of her kingdom on her shoulders without faltering–that pulls me toward her, even when I know she wants nothing to do with me. And maybe that's part of the problem. I've spent so much of my life being wanted, being admired, that I don't know how to handle being dismissed.

"River, are you even paying attention?" Maerilee's voice cuts through my thoughts, sharp and annoyed.

I glance up, realizing the group has stopped. She's staring at me, her silver eyes narrowed, her hands on her hips.

"What?" I snap, the bitterness in my tone more reflex than intention.

"We're deciding which path to take," she says, exasperation lacing her words. "Maybe if you weren't so busy brooding, you'd have something useful to contribute."

There she goes again, berating me for no good reason. So what if I'm not contributing? She wouldn't listen to my opinion if I did.

The others exchange glances, and I can feel their judgment, their silent agreement with her assessment. Heat rises in my chest, a mix of anger and humiliation, but I don't say anything. What's the point? No matter what I do, it's never enough for her.

As the group moves forward, I hang back, my thoughts spiraling. What am I even doing here? I've already lost everything–my title, my family, my home. And for what? To be part of a group where I'm barely tolerated? To chase after someone who doesn't even like me?

The thought of walking away, leaving all of this behind, finding some corner of the world where I can start over, where I can be something more than a disgraced prince crosses my mind.

But then I remember what happened when Permiton left. Without him, Maerilee's power weakened. If I leave, she won't have the strength she needs to protect Altinna. And no matter how angry or bitter I feel, I can't do that to her. I can't do that to any of them.

Still, the frustration festers, growing with each passing moment, until I can't hold it in any longer. As the group stops to rest by a small stream, I approach Maerilee, my steps deliberate, my chest tight with the weight of everything I need to say.

"I need to speak with you," I say, my voice tense.

She looks up from where she's crouched by the water, her expression wary. "What is it, River?"

I gesture for her to step away from the others, and after a moment's hesitation, she follows me a few paces down the trail. Her arms are crossed when she stops, her posture defensive, and it only stokes the fire inside me.

"What am I supposed to get out of all this?" I ask, the bitterness in my voice sharper than I intended. "I've given up everything for you, Maerilee. I turned my back on my parents, on my kingdom, on my whole damn future, and for what? To be treated like a burden? To be ignored and insulted at every turn? I'd just like to know how the hell it benefits me to stay."

Her eyes flash with anger, and she takes a step closer, her voice low and fierce. "Are you seriously complaining right now? Do you even hear yourself? You're so self-centered that you can't even imagine doing something for the good of someone else."

"I'm just saying—"

"No, you're not *just saying*," she snaps, cutting me off. "You're whining. You think you're the only one who's lost something? My kingdom is likely at war with your people as we speak. My mother is dying, and every second we spend out here is a second closer to losing her. And you're worried about what you're 'supposed to get out of this'? Are you kidding me?"

Her words hit like a slap, each one cutting deeper than the last. I open my mouth to respond, but she doesn't give me the chance.

"You get out of this what you put into it, River," she continues, her voice trembling with anger. "And so far, you've put in nothing. You've done nothing but complain and make things harder for everyone. If you want to be part of this, if you want to matter, then start acting like it. Stop thinking about what you're losing, and start thinking about what you can give."

I take a step back, the weight of her words crashing over me. She's right, of course. I've been selfish, too caught up in my own misery to see the bigger picture. But hearing it from her, spoken with such raw emotion, cuts deeper than I ever expected.

"I'm sorry," I say finally, my voice quiet. "You're right."

Her anger seems to falter at my words, and she exhales slowly, the tension in her shoulders easing slightly. "Good. Then prove it."

She turns and walks back to the group, leaving me standing there, my thoughts a tangled mess. I watch her go, the fire in her step, the determination in every movement, and I feel something shift inside me. She's not just some prize to be won, some challenge to conquer. She's a force of nature, and if I want to be part of her world, I need to be worthy of it.

I take a deep breath, the anger and frustration fading, replaced by a quiet resolve. I don't know what the future holds, but I know one thing—I'm not walking away, not from this, and not from her.

As I return to the group, I catch Brook watching me, his expression unreadable. For once, I don't feel the need to say anything, to assert myself or prove a point. I just take my place among them, ready to face whatever comes next.

21

ALL OUR STRENGTH

Maerilee

The sun shines down brightly on us as we press forward, the air thick with the promise of something monumental just ahead. My chest feels heavy, not from the climb or the journey, but from the weight of everything riding on us reaching Bright Waters. Time feels like a noose tightening around my neck, pulling tighter with every passing moment. This journey has already taken much longer than I'd ever anticipated. If we don't get back to Altinna soon, I fear what we'll find when we return.

Brook walks by my side, quiet but focused. Recently, I've come to rely on his calm, steady presence, in his new sense of confidence and authority. And now, my heart swells with the love I have for him, something I did not expect at all. It took me by surprise, knocking the wind out of me, but it makes trusting him, relying on him, that much easier.

"How much further?" I ask, my voice a whisper against the rustling leaves.

Brook glances at me, a faint smile tugging at his lips. "Less than a day, my love," he whispers back, brushing his arm against mine. "We're almost there."

Relief washes over me, but it's fleeting. "Less than a day," I murmur, as though saying it aloud will make it go by faster. "And once we reach the springs, then what?"

"Then we harness the power of Bright Waters," he says simply. "And go back to Altinna. The journey home should be less perilous. All of these trials have been meant to test us, but legend says that leaving is a much simpler feat. We'll be back to Altinna in no time."

I can't help the laugh that escapes me, soft and tinged with disbelief. "When you lay it out like that, it all sounds so easy."

"I said 'should,' didn't I?" he chuckles, completely at ease. "I'm not making any promises."

The group trudges along behind us, each lost in their own thoughts. Akin is as watchful as ever, his gaze darting to every shadow as though danger might leap from the trees at any moment. River's usual arrogance has dimmed, replaced by a quiet brooding that makes me wonder what's going through his mind. Permiton, of course, remains aloof from the others, his steps measured and precise, as though he knows exactly what lies ahead.

"We're not done yet," Brook says suddenly, his voice pulling me back to the present. "There are two more barriers left to cross before we reach the springs."

I stop, turning to face him fully. "Two more? What kind of barriers?"

He shakes his head, his brow furrowing. "I don't know exactly. The texts I read were vague, more like legends than instructions. But what I do know is that the barriers are meant to test us."

"Test us how?" River asks from behind, his tone edged with impatience. "Because if it's more climbing, I'm out."

Brook gives him a look, the kind he's perfected over years of enduring his brother's antics. "The remaining barriers aren't physical. They're magical. They're meant to challenge us, to see if we're worthy of Bright Waters."

"Worthy," Permiton echoes, his voice thoughtful. "Interesting choice of word."

I glance at him, a flicker of unease tightening in my chest. "What do you mean?"

"Bright Waters isn't just a source of magic," Permiton explains. "It's a gatekeeper. It chooses who can access its power and who can't. These barriers, whatever they entail, are designed to reveal our true selves, to test our resolve."

The weight of his words settles over the group like a heavy blanket, and I feel my stomach twist. I've faced so much on this journey already, fought against my own fears, my doubts, my weaknesses, but the thought of being tested again, of being judged, fills me with dread. It hasn't gone so well for me lately.

"We'll face it together," Akin says firmly, his voice cutting through the silence. "Whatever these barriers are, we'll get through them."

His words bring a flicker of comfort, but it's fleeting. I nod, forcing myself to focus on the path ahead. "Let's keep moving," I command, walking faster with anticipation. The sooner we get there, the sooner this will all be over with, and we can go home.

The terrain grows steeper as we climb, the air cooler, sharper, as though we're nearing the heart of something ancient and powerful. As the hours pass, I find myself walking closer to Akin, his steady presence a balm to my fraying nerves. He doesn't say much, but I can feel his eyes on me, protective and reassuring. It's a comfort I didn't realize I needed until now.

"I'm scared," I admit quietly, the words slipping out before I can stop them.

Akin glances at me, his expression softening. "You're allowed to be scared, Maerilee," he says kindly. "But don't let it stop you."

I nod, his words sinking into me like an anchor, grounding me. "Thank you."

He squeezes my shoulder briefly, a silent gesture of support, before returning his focus to the path ahead. It's a small moment, but it bolsters me, gives me the strength to keep going.

Brook pauses suddenly, holding up a hand to signal us to stop. "We're close," he says, his voice low. "The next barrier is just ahead."

My heart pounds as I follow his gaze, my eyes landing on a shimmering veil of light stretching across the path. It's beautiful and otherworldly, but there's an edge to it, a sense of danger that makes my skin prickle.

"What do we do?" I ask, my voice barely above a whisper.

Brook steps forward, his hands outstretched, his magic already beginning to flow.

"We figure out what it is and what it requires of us."

* * *

PERMITON

THE MOMENT WE COME UPON THE BARRIER, I KNOW IT'S GOING TO BE A problem. The air ahead shimmers, faint and rippling, like heat rising from the stones on a summer day. But there's nothing warm about this magic. It hums with tension, crackling like a storm waiting to break, an ancient and powerful magic that I doubt any of the others have ever encountered before.

They're young, practically children. This is nothing they'd be familiar with. Still, I have to rely on our collective strength. They may not know how to handle this magic, but it's our bond together that makes us powerful. I know that we're capable of breaking this barrier. We just have to do it together.

I step forward cautiously, the weight of the barrier's power pressing against my senses. It's old, far older than anything I've worked with before, and layered with complexities that make my head ache just looking at it. This is no simple barrier. It's a protection spell, ancient and intricate, designed to repel even the most skilled magic users. No wonder so many assume Bright Waters is a myth. I doubt many have ever gotten this far on their quest.

The group gathers behind me, watching, their anticipation thick in the air. I glance back at them, at their expectant faces, and feel the familiar weight of responsibility settle over me. They're counting on me to figure this out, to get us through. Even if they still doubt me, I am the only one qualified to do this.

"Permiton?" Maerilee's voice is quiet, but there's an edge of urgency to it. "What is it? How can we help?"

"It's a very complicated protection spell," I explain, turning my attention back to the barrier. "A powerful one. It's meant to keep out anyone who doesn't belong."

Brook steps forward, his brows furrowed.

"Will you be able to break it?" he asks, his tone clear that he's ready to step in if he's needed. He has proved useful so far, but I don't think even he is capable of handling this.

"I'm going to try," I say, my tone more confident than I feel. "But it's not going to be easy. I need to tap into our collective strength for this."

"Of course you do," I hear River mutter under his breath, though it's clear it's not his intent for anyone to overhear him. He's just being his usual snarky self.

I reach out, letting my magic flow toward the barrier, feeling for its structure, its weaknesses. The spell resists immediately, pushing back with a force that makes me stagger. I grit my teeth, steadying myself, and dig deeper, unraveling the threads of magic one by one.

The spell is layered in a way that's almost beautiful, each thread woven into the next with precision and care. It's a masterpiece, really, and I can't help but feel a grudging respect for the caster who created it. It's nearly as impenetrable as the barrier around Altinna used to be.

But admiration won't get us through.

"Permiton, how can we help? What do you need from us?" Akin asks, his voice steady and practical. I'm grateful for it, even more grateful that he seems to have forgiven me.

"I need more power," I say simply. "This spell is too strong for me to break alone. I'll need all of you."

Without hesitation, the group steps closer, forming a loose circle around me. Maerilee reaches out first, her hand brushing my arm as her magic flows into me, warm and steady. The others follow, their power joining hers, a mix of strength and support that bolsters mine.

With their magic reinforcing mine, I dive back into the spell, pulling at its threads, unraveling its layers. It's like untangling a knot the size of a mountain, slow, painstaking work that requires focus and precision. The spell fights me every step of the way, its resistance growing stronger the deeper I go.

Sweat beads on my forehead, and my hands tremble as I weave our collective magic into the spell, forcing it to bend to my will. The strain is almost unbearable, the weight of the magic pressing down on me like a physical force. But I can't give up, not when we're this close.

Maerilee is counting on me.

"Permiton," Maerilee says softly, her voice a lifeline in the chaos. "You can do this. We're all here for you."

I nod, unable to speak, and push harder, my magic surging through the barrier's defenses. The spell falters, its structure weakening, and I seize the opportunity, tearing through its core with everything I have.

The barrier shatters with a sound like breaking glass, the shimmering light dissolving into the air. My companions collapse to the ground, covering their heads as if there is physically glass shattering around them.

For a moment, there's silence, the tension hanging thick around us. When it's clear what has happened, the group exhales collectively, realizing they're safe and we're one barrier closer to the waters.

I stagger back, my legs threatening to give out beneath me. Maerilee is there instantly, her hands steadying me as I sink to the ground. My chest heaves with effort, all of my energy drained from my body.

"Are you okay?" she asks, her voice laced with concern as her hand moves to my forehead, gently pressing the back of it against me like my mother did so many years ago.

"I'll be fine," I manage, though my head throbs and my vision swims. "It took more out of me than I expected."

Akin kneels beside me, his expression unreadable but his presence grounding. "Thank you," he says simply.

I nod, the weight of the moment settling over me. The barrier is gone, and the path ahead is clear for now. But I know there's more to come, more challenges that will test us in ways we can't yet imagine.

"Thank you," Maerilee says softly, her gaze steady on mine. "We couldn't have done this without you."

Her words hit me harder than I expect, a strange mix of pride and guilt twisting in my chest. I nod again, unable to meet her eyes, and I focus on catching my breath.

As the group begins to move forward, I take a moment to center myself, drawing on what little reserves of strength I have left. The spell is broken, but the journey isn't over. Bright Waters is still ahead, its power waiting to be claimed.

2 2

THE GUARDIAN

THE AIR SHIFTS AS WE CROSS THROUGH THE REMNANTS OF THE BARRIER, its hum of magic dissipating behind us. For a moment, I can only focus on the ache in my legs and the burn in my lungs, the physical strain of the journey catching up to me. But as the path widens, my breath catches for an entirely different reason.

Past the barrier Permiton's just broken is a large, expansive grotto. It stretches before us, a breathtaking expanse of green and blue, shimmering like something out of a dream. A massive waterfall cascades from the mountain above, its waters glowing faintly in the dim light. The air is thick with moisture, cool and refreshing, and the sound of the rushing water drowns out everything else.

A sound like rumbling rocks comes from behind us, and we turn to see that the barrier we've just come through is back up. My heart falls, crushed by the thought that we'll have to go through that again. Though Permiton did most of the work, he still drew a lot of power from all of us. I'm not even sure we have the strength to go back through. What if we're trapped here? Perhaps that's the reason so many people think the waters are a myth.

As if reading my thoughts, Permiton comes up behind me and places a weak hand on my shoulder.

"It's just a protection from outside forces," he tells me, his voice faltering from exhaustion. "The trials are meant to keep people out, but the waters aren't going to let us stay. As soon as we have what we need, we'll be directed right back to the ruins."

"Thank the gods," I murmur, unable to even comprehend what the journey back entails. All I want is a hot meal and a soft bed, though I have a feeling neither is in my near future.

"Bright Waters," Brook murmurs somewhere to my left, his voice tinged with awe. "I can't believe we're here."

He stands completely still, his eyes taking in the scenery. Unshed tears form in his eyes, and he falters. I turn to see Akin and Maerilee have similar looks of wonderment on their faces. Permiton leaves my side and finds a rock to rest on, his strength clearly gone.

Even I can't muster a snarky response to all of this. The sight of the waters is absolutely indescribable. I've spent my entire life surrounded by water, raised in a kingdom built on its magic, but this feels almost holy. It's ancient, untouched by the fae, radiating a power so pure it makes the hairs on the back of my neck stand on end.

"It's magnificent," Maerilee says softly, her voice breaking the spell that seems to have fallen over all of us. She steps forward, her silver hair catching the faint light as she takes it all in, her eyes wide with wonder. A smile breaks over her face, the first genuine smile I've seen with her on this whole journey.

Akin's usual stoicism is softened by quiet reverence, and even Permiton seems affected, his gaze thoughtful as he studies the waterfall. It's rare for our group to share a moment of silence like this, and it feels strange to all seemingly be feeling the same thing. It's as if, in this moment, we're truly one. It's unsettling.

"All right," I say, breaking the silence. "We're finally here. Now what are we supposed to do?"

Brook turns to me, his expression serious and annoyed. I'm still not used to the boldness of his disdain toward me. He used to be much quieter and subversive.

"There's still one more barrier," he says, a sharp edge to his voice.

I bristle at his tone and frown, gesturing toward the water. "This is it, isn't it?" I ask, feeling somewhat petulant. "This is the famed Bright Waters. We've made it. We should just take what we need and go."

Brook shakes his head. "The waters are here, yes, but there's one final trial before we can access their power. The guardians will test us."

"Guardians?" I repeat, the word sitting uneasily in my mouth. "What kind of guardians?"

I glance around us, at the endless expanse of trees and sky. There's nothing around us that I can see, but there could very well be sprites in the trees. I take a defensive position, trying to draw on my magic for protection, but I'm still weakened by Permiton's spell.

Brook hesitates, his brow furrowing. "I'm not exactly sure," he admits, sounding humbler now. Good. "The texts weren't clear on the details, only that they protect the waters and judge those who seek them."

"Right," I mutter, already feeling my irritation rise. "So we're just supposed to stand around and wait for some mystical test to come to us? Or worse, attack us? We're not going to survive another blow."

I don't relax my position, still ready for attack. No one else seems to be worried about it, though. Even Akin seems relaxed, his sword still sheathed at his side. I can't understand their ease. If someone is going to test us, we have to prepare. It's about time we finally get this mission over with and get the hell out of Oceana before we're killed.

"Patience, River," Permiton says from his perch, his voice annoyingly calm. "Rushing in without understanding what we're dealing with would be unwise."

I roll my eyes, the tension in my chest building. I've been patient. I've endured a thousand indignities on this journey, not least of which was being captured by the army that once bowed down to me. I've watched Maerilee draw closer to each one of these men while I've been left out in the cold. My patience is officially gone. I'm ready to have this all over with.

"Maybe," I say dismissively. "But standing here isn't going to get us anywhere."

Ignoring the others' protests, I step forward, my boots crunching across the gravel as I approach the river. The water glows faintly, its surface shimmering with a strange, iridescent light. It's mesmerizing, pulling me closer despite the unease prickling at the back of my mind.

"River, stop," Maerilee calls, her tone sharp with warning.

I glance back at her, a smirk tugging at my lips. "Relax, Princess," I chide, not displeased by how concerned she looks for me. About time. "It's just water, after all. I'm the prince of this land-"

"Former prince," Brook is all too quick to chime in.

"The waters still obey me, even if my people no longer do," I continue, ignoring my brother.

"Don't be an idiot," Akin growls, his hand already on the hilt of his sword. "You don't know what you're dealing with." He tugs on his sword, and for a moment, I think he might pull it out to fight me. It wouldn't be the first time. I shrug him off, though, unwilling to let a guard tell me what to do.

"Maybe not," I admit, turning back to the river, "but someone has to take the first step."

As I reach the edge of the water, the air around me seems to shift, growing heavier, charged with a power that makes my skin crawl. I pause, my instincts screaming at me to turn back, but I push the feeling aside. I've come this far, and I'll be damned if I let fear stop me now.

The moment my foot touches the water's edge, a sharp pain explodes in my shoulder. I cry out, stumbling backward as the force of the impact drives me to my knees. My hand flies to the source of the pain, my fingers brushing against the shaft of an arrow embedded in my flesh.

"What the—" I begin, but my words die in my throat as the water ripples, and a figure rises from its depths.

The water doesn't even break as the giant figure appears from the surface, almost as if it's part of the water itself. The guardian is unlike anything I've ever seen, its form half human and half beast. Its skin glistens with the same iridescent sheen as the water, and its eyes glow with an intense, unearthly light. It holds a bow in its hands, another arrow already nocked and aimed directly at me.

Its hollow eyes keep me rooted to this spot, the pain in my shoulder not remotely comparing to the curiosity and fear I simultaneously feel. The guardian's power radiates off it so strongly it feels like it's physically pressing down on me, drowning me though I'm breathing air. At the same time, I can feel my own power draining as if it's taking it away from me little by little.

In a flash, I'm a child again, sitting in my bed as my mother reads me a story to help me fall asleep.

"Bright Waters is the source of all of our powers," she says, her voice both light and warning. "Don't take that for granted, my boy. If the waters find you unworthy, they can strip those powers away forever, leaving you a broken fae."

All those stories I took for granted, all that power I assumed was mine for the taking. It feels like it's leaking out of me, flowing from my body into the river itself. I've never felt so weak, so vulnerable in my entire life. A thought flashes through my mind violently and clearly. I'm going to die here. This is the end of my journey.

"Stay back!" Maerilee screams, her voice ringing out as the guardian steps closer, its movements fluid and deliberate.

It turns its attention away from me, and I suddenly feel like myself again, the weight of its power easing off as it sets its sight on another target. Maerilee. I still feel weak, but I'm able to move again, able to see what's about to happen, almost as if it's happening in slow motion.

The guardian pulls back its bowstring, the target changed from me to her. It's not going to miss. I feel it in my bones. Pain radiates from my shoulder, but I force myself to my feet, my heart pounding as the guardian's gaze locks onto Maerilee. It raises its bow, the arrow shifting to point at her chest.

"No!" I scream, adrenaline surging through me as I lunge forward, throwing myself between her and the guardian. The second arrow strikes me just below the collarbone, its force driving me to the ground. The pain is blinding, white-hot, and I can feel my strength slipping away with every passing second.

"River!" Maerilee's voice is distant, muffled, as though I'm hearing it through a thick fog. I try to move, to push myself up, but my body refuses to obey. The world tilts and blurs, the edges of my vision darkening.

I can feel her hands on me, her voice frantic as she calls my name, but it's not enough to anchor me. The pain fades, replaced by a strange, numbing cold, and I realize I'm slipping away into nothingness.

Memories flash before my eyes in quick succession with no seeming pattern or order. My mother and father bring a babbling baby Brook to meet me, and I immediately feel jealous of him. I vow to make sure he always knows his place in the world. Faces of women I've seduced breeze by like ghosts, reminding me how I always treated them as commodities, challenges.

I'm meeting Maerilee, taken aback by her brazenness and rejection. We're kissing for the first time, our power surging together like nothing I've felt before. I know that she's my One, as much as we would both like it to be untrue. I watch as she falls in love with Brook, as her bond with Akin grows, as she chooses to trust Permiton after his betrayal. And through it all, I can't help but think, if only I'd put my pride aside, maybe she could have loved me, too.

Maybe she will once I'm gone.

The last thing I see is Maerilee's face, her silver eyes filled with fear and something else I can't quite name. I want to tell her it's all right, that I'm going to be okay, but the words don't come.

And then there's nothing.

23

WORDS UNSPOKEN

Maerilee

THE WORLD AROUND ME BLURS INTO CHAOS AS THE GUARDIAN RISES from the water, its iridescent form casting a ghostly glow over the riverbank. It advances toward our group, though it seems done with me now that River has been shot. I hear the sharp, metallic twang of arrows and the clash of magic as Akin and Brook fight it off, but my focus is solely on River.

He's sprawled on the ground, his face pale and his chest heaving as blood pours from his wounds. I pull the arrows out as gently as possible, but all that seems to do is make him bleed more .Pressing desperately against his chest, I try to staunch the flow, but the crimson warmth seeps through my fingers, relentless and terrifying. I can't make it stop, and he's fading fast.

"Stay with me, River," I demand, my voice trembling. "Please, don't do this."

His skin is cold to the touch, his breaths shallow and ragged, raspy and labored. Panic claws at my chest, threatening to choke me, but I force myself to focus. I tear a strip of cloth from my tunic, pressing it against the wound near his heart, but it's not enough. The blood keeps coming, pooling around us and staining the grass a dark, sickening red.

"Damn it, River! Don't you dare die on me!" My voice cracks as tears blur my vision. "Why did you have to be so reckless?"

Behind me, I hear the sounds of battle. Akin sharply commands the other two as they attack the guardian on three fronts. Brook's water magic seems to do little against the guardian's attacks. Permiton is still sitting on a perch, reciting some incantation to keep the creature away. They're fighting to keep us safe, to drive the guardian back, but I can't bring myself to look away from River. His life is slipping through my fingers, and I can't stop it.

I hear a loud roar and look up to see the guardian surrendering, fading back into the waters as if it never existed, as if it didn't try to kill River. I meet its eyes before its head sinks below the surface of the water. Though they're clear, it's as if I feel them approving of me, silently communicating that it's found me favorable. A chill runs through my body as the waters completely envelop it and then everything goes still.

"Maerilee, move!" Brook's voice cuts through my reverie, urgent and commanding. I glance up to see him rushing toward us, his hands cupped and glowing faintly with magic. He kneels beside me, his expression tight with determination.

"What are you doing?" I ask, my voice breaking as I clutch at River's still form.

"Trust me," Brook says simply, his voice steady. He holds his hands over River's chest, the water gathered in his palms shimmering with an otherworldly light. With a fluid motion, he pours the water over River's wounds, and I watch, breathless, as the liquid seeps into his skin.

At first, nothing happens, and my heart sinks, hopelessness spreading through my body as I realize that all of this has been for nothing. If the waters can't even heal River, whose wounds are fresh, how will they help my mother?

But then, slowly, the bleeding begins to stop. The torn flesh knits itself back together, the angry redness fading to pale scars that glisten faintly in the light like silver. I stare in awe, my tears flowing freely now, but this time they're tears of hope.

"How?" I whisper, unable to finish the question.

Brook doesn't answer immediately, his focus entirely on his brother. His hands tremble slightly as he channels the last of the water's magic, his face pale but resolute. When the wounds are fully closed, he leans back, his shoulders sagging with exhaustion.

"It's the waters," he says finally, his voice hoarse as he collapses on the ground and swipes at his eyes. "It's nice to see that the legends are actually true."

I nod at his words as I wipe my own face, too overcome with emotion to speak. I look down at River, his chest rising and falling steadily now, his face still pale but no longer deathly. Relief crashes over me, leaving me weak and trembling. I clutch his hand, holding it tightly as if that alone will keep him tethered to life.

"Thank you," I whisper, my voice breaking. "Thank you, Brook."

He nods, his expression softening as he meets my gaze.

"I couldn't let my brother die," he says with a shrug, his voice thick with emotion. "He might be the biggest pain in the ass, but I'd rather him be a living pain in the ass. And, after all, he saved your life."

The reality of what happened hits me like a tidal wave. River stepped in front of the guardian's arrow for me. He threw himself into harm's way, sacrificing himself without hesitation. My heart clenches at the thought, a mix of gratitude and guilt washing over me.

"We need to set up camp," Akin says, his voice cutting through the quiet that's fallen over us. He stands a few feet away, his sword sheathed but his stance still tense, his eyes scanning the surroundings for any further threats. "River's not going anywhere until he's fully healed."

I nod, unable to tear my gaze away from River as the others move to set up camp near the water. Akin and Permiton work together to gather supplies while Brook and I spread out blankets and prepare a space for River to rest.

Once our shelter is built, I stay by his side, refusing to leave even for a moment. I brush his hair away from his forehead, my fingers trembling as I trace the lines of his face. He looks so vulnerable like this, so unlike the stubborn, arrogant prince who's been a thorn in my side since the moment we met.

The others make food, eat, settle in for the night, but I barely notice as the hours pass by. The ethereal glow of day turns into a mystical night, a large moon hanging overhead, watching us. I barely notice any of it, the world around me fading into the background as I keep vigil over him. The others move about quietly, their voices low as they discuss our next steps, but I don't listen. My entire focus is on River, on the steady rise and fall of his chest, on the faint warmth returning to his skin.

When his eyes finally flutter open sometime in the middle of the night, I feel a wave of relief so intense it leaves me breathless.

"River," I say softly, leaning closer as his gaze finds mine. "You're awake."

He blinks slowly, his expression dazed as he methodically takes in our surroundings.

"What happened?"

"You saved me," I say, my voice trembling with emotion. "You threw yourself in front of the guardian's arrow to protect me."

His brow furrows, as if trying to piece together the events that led us here.

"That doesn't sound like me at all," he mutters, his tone laced with confusion and a hint of amusement. "It shot me?"

"Twice," I confirm, a shaky laugh escaping me despite myself. "But you're okay now. Brook healed you with the water's magic."

His eyes sweep around our tiny shelter to find his brother, but he's made his own shelter a few feet away from us, out of sight. River turns back to me, his usual bravado dimmed by the lingering exhaustion in his eyes.

"You're okay?" he asks, his voice quieter now as he takes one of my hands in his.

"I'm fine," I assure him, clutching him. "Thanks to you. But why, River? Why did you save me?"

His jaw tightens, his gaze flickering away for a moment before returning to mine. He sits up slowly, so that we're face to face.

"You know why," he answers hoarsely, his other hand tracing my forehead.

I stare at him, my heart pounding as his words sink in. He holds my gaze for a moment longer, and I nod, suddenly aware of our proximity to one another. He leans in slowly, gently, and I reflexively match his movements until our lips are pressed together in a gentle kiss.

He traces his fingers down my face, my neck, then moves back to my hair until he's gripping the back of my neck, putting all of his emotions into the embrace. It's as if he's using his kisses to say the words he can't bring himself to say.

I do the same, whether out of my own pride or an inability to truly name what it is I'm feeling. In all this time we've known each other, I've viewed River as an inconvenience, as a piece of my puzzle that didn't quite fit like the others. Though he proved his loyalty by standing up to his parents, it never occurred to me that he felt anything other than obligation, or perhaps a desire for more power.

Yet, as his tongue slips into my mouth, and his hands trail lower, gripping my waist, I realize that his feelings must run deeper. Certainly deeper than he's willing to admit. Maybe he never will. Maybe I never will either. But almost losing him today clarified how much he belongs by my side.

I settle back against the pallet of blankets, pulling him down on top of me. He balances himself on his elbow while his other hand trails at the hem of my tunic, awaiting permission. I grab his hand, pulling it under until his fingers are ghosting over my breasts, my skin prickling with desire. A quiet moan escapes my lips as he gently squeezes my nipple, forcing me to arch my back against him.

I feel his evident desire pressing against me as the heat between us grows, but he doesn't push me. Instead, he lavishes me with his affection, as if it's his only goal. And maybe, for once, it is.

I place a hand on his chest and gently push him away as the image of the arrow striking him plays in my head. He immediately stops, tensing up as he pulls away.

"I'm sorry," he says, coughing to hide his emotion. "That was stupid, I shouldn't have done that."

He tries to move away from me, but I grab his wrist to hold him in place. He's sitting back up now, not looking at me, but I move into his lap, straddling him and forcing him to meet my gaze.

"I wanted you to," I whisper as I gently place a kiss on his lips. His hands move back to my hips as if by their own volition. His expression remains guarded, though. "I only stopped you to make sure you were okay."

His eyes soften, and a small, cocky smile breaks over his face. So he hasn't changed too much.

"I've never been better," he answers, pulling my bottom lip between his teeth. My hips rock against his hardness, and he hisses. "Although, I wouldn't say no to you taking off your clothes."

A lightness washes over me, and I can't help but giggle at his tone. Something has irrevocably shifted between us, and I realize that I actually like River. One day, I could potentially even love him. He still has some growing to do, but he's shown me today that he is capable of it.

Wordlessly, I stand, slowly fidgeting with the buttons of my tunic. I shed out of my clothes until I'm bare before him, my skin glistening in the moonlight that seeps in between the leaves of our little shelter. He breathes out a small sigh that very much sounds like the word "wow" and traces his hands over my legs, my thighs, my hips, until he's gently tugging me back down to him.

He kisses me more urgently, as his hands roam over my skin, and I can feel the wet heat growing between my legs.

"I need you," I moan, ripping at his shirt until it falls off him, his quiet laughter circling us.

"You have me," he whispers, as he moves me back to the ground, hovering over me as he shrugs out of his trousers. With a swift motion, he positions himself at my entrance and thrusts in, somehow lighting up every nerve inside of me.

I see stars as he begins to move inside of me, his rhythm slow and deliberate. We take our time, as if we have an abundance of it. He traces patterns on my arm, along my breasts, on the insides of my thighs. My body trembles at each touch, the pleasure building in my core. He pulls me apart like a loose thread on a gown until I'm totally unraveling, my body thrashing beneath him as I bite my tongue to stay quiet.

He holds me tightly as we fall apart together, shuddering and panting from the exertion. I can barely move after, but he pulls a blanket over and holds me. For the first time since he was wounded, I feel tethered back to the earth then feel the darkness of sleep pull me under.

24

UNWELCOME GUESTS

Maerilee

THE MORNING LIGHT FILTERS THROUGH THE CANOPY OF TREES, CASTING soft golden rays over our little shelter. Through the leaves, I can see the waters shimmer, still and peaceful, as though they've forgotten the chaos of the day before. River is still sleeping soundly, his arm draped around me as his chest slowly rises and falls. There's nothing left on his skin but a faint silver line from where his wound healed.

I carefully extract myself from his arms, surprised at how reluctant I feel to leave him. His face is peaceful, an innocent smile playing on his lips as he dreams. I place a gentle, chaste kiss on his forehead before I dress.

Once I'm decent, I go to stand at the edge of the river, the sound of the waterfall a soothing backdrop, but my mind is anything but calm. Something inside of me has irrevocably changed since this journey began. It isn't just my relationships with my Four, but there's a growing power deep inside of me that wasn't there before.

I hold my hand out over the water and watch as it gently ripples under my power. Testing, I focus my magic outward, creating a protection spell that encompasses all of my sleeping companions. Strangely, though, it stops just at the edge of the waters, as if they are immune to any outside magic. For all I know, they are.

Brook emerges from his shelter, his expression thoughtful as he kneels by the water's edge. I retract my barrier before he notices and watch as he dips his fingers into the glowing current, the soft light reflecting in his dark eyes.

"According to the legends," he begins, his voice still slightly scratchy from sleep, "each of us is allowed to take one vial of the waters. No more."

I hum thoughtfully at this then realize why he's telling me. He used the water to save River yesterday. He won't be able to take any more. My heart lurches as I consider the sacrifice he made for his brother. He would have already known this when he took the water, but he didn't care. He stands up and shakes the water off his hands. I pull him into an embrace, thanking him for saving River. When we move away, we're both glassy-eyed from unshed tears.

Slowly, the other men wake up, and soon we are all gathered at the banks of Bright Waters, hanging on Brook's every word as he tells us childhood stories about the waters. River, I notice, is silent and paying rapt attention. After what happened yesterday, he seems almost humbled. He meets my gaze briefly, a flicker of something unspoken passing between us, and smiles wickedly before looking away. I feel a fluttering in my stomach, surprised by how my feelings have grown in a day. Then again, maybe they were always under the surface, just waiting to be released.

"What will happen if someone tries to take more than one vial?" Akin asks, his tone sharp and wary as Brook repeats what he told me earlier.

"The guardian will return," Brook says darkly. He straightens, brushing his hands on his trousers. "And I doubt it will be as lenient this time."

"Lenient?" River mutters under his breath, though there's no heat to his words. He raises his hands in mock surrender. "All right, point taken. I'll listen from now on. No more playing hero; no more testing ancient magical waters. Got it."

Brook's lips quirk in a faint smile, but he doesn't comment. Instead, he retrieves a small glass vial from his bag and holds it up, its surface catching the light.

"I can't take any more for myself," he says, his voice quieter now. "I've already used the waters to save River." He hesitates, glancing at his brother. River's brow furrows, and he nods once, a seriousness settling over him.

"You have my word, brother," he says earnestly. "I'll keep my vial safe for you. If anything happens to you, I've got your back."

Something shifts in the air between them, an unspoken understanding that feels sacred in its own way. Akin looks between them in shock, but Permiton smiles in his knowing, omniscient way. None of us have seen this side of River before. He's acting loyal, protective, even selfless. It makes my chest ache in a way I don't quite understand.

Brook passes out the remaining vials, each of us holding one carefully, almost reverently.

I kneel by the water, dipping my vial into the glowing current. I can feel its power hum beneath my fingertips. It's alive, ancient and pure, and it fills me with a sense of awe I can't put into words. As I cap my vial, I watch as Akin, Permiton, and River all have similar experiences as they encounter the waters.

When we're finished, Brook straightens and glances around at the group.

"We have what we came for," he says. "Now, it's time to go."

There's a weight to his words, a finality that makes my stomach twist. This journey has changed us all in ways I'm still trying to process, and the thought of leaving this sacred place feels almost bittersweet. But with that feeling comes an anxiousness to get back to my mother–finally. Now I have the power to save her.

We gather our things in silence, preparing for the long journey back to Altinna. Yet as we step out of the grotto and back into the haze, something strange happens. The landscape around us shifts, the trees dissolving into mist, and when the haze clears, we're standing at the edge of the ruins where this leg of our journey began.

"What? How?" Akin stutters, his hand instinctively going to his sword.

Permiton shrugs, a faint smile playing at his lips. "The magic of the waters," he says simply. "They brought us back. I told you they would," he directs to River.

River lets out a low whistle, glancing around with an expression that's equal parts impressed and unsettled. "I guess that's our cue. They're telling us we don't have to go home, but we sure as hell can't stay here."

I can't help but laugh at his newfound levity, and Akin eyes me suspiciously. This new dynamic is going to take some getting used to for all of us.

I glance back toward the path we came from, but the grotto is gone, replaced by the same thick mist as before. It feels like a dream, like the last few days were nothing but a vivid illusion. But the weight of the vial in my hand, the faint glow of its contents, reminds me that it was real. All of it. At some point or another, we all could have died. Yet we made it through together, and we've come out even stronger.

"We should keep moving," Akin says, his voice cutting through the quiet. He steps forward, his gaze scanning the horizon. "The sooner we're back in Altinna, the better."

I nod, my mind now solely focused on my mother. It will take another few days to get out of Oceana, and that's assuming we don't have any more run-ins with the army or Commander Heela. I'm not afraid, though. My powers are stronger than they've ever been, and I know that I can protect us if things get dicey.

We follow Akin, the ruins fading into the background as we make our way toward the edge of the barrier that marks the waters' protection. My thoughts are heavy, swirling with everything we've been through, everything that still lies ahead. I clutch the vial tightly. It's a tangible reminder of the stakes we're facing. If Mother dies, the barrier around Altinna will fall. I may be stronger now, but I'm not nearly strong enough to re-erect the barrier around the whole kingdom.

As we step over the threshold of Bright Waters, the air shifts again, becoming colder and sharper, and I feel a prickle of unease crawl up my spine. The moment we're fully out of its protection, we realize we're not alone.

Figures emerge from the shadows, their movements swift and deliberate. At first, I think it's the Oceanean army, but I soon realize it's the rebels. They fan out, surrounding us with a precision that makes my heart pound. Their weapons gleam in the light, and their faces are grim, determined.

"Stand your ground," Akin says, his voice low and commanding as he draws his sword. The rest of us fall into a loose formation, ready to fight despite the exhaustion weighing on us.

Caelan steps forward, his eyes narrowing as he takes us in. "Well, well," he says, his tone impressed. "It seems you were right. Bright Waters is real."

"Let us pass," River growls, taking on his authoritative, princely tone. To my ears, he sounds like the same prince I met at the ball, but my heart knows differently. He's changed.

My heart races, but I force myself to meet Caelan's gaze, to stand tall despite the anxiety clawing at my chest.

My power shoots out of me like a bolt of lightning, and before I even comprehend it, I see that I've projected a firm barrier around us, perfectly placed between our group and the rebels.

In all of my imaginings of what could go wrong on our journey home, I hadn't even considered the rebels would get in our way. They're supposed to be on our side, fighting for Altinna. Rage bubbles up inside of me, and I know that I could happily take it out on any of these men in hand to hand combat, if only to release my anger.

But Permiton comes to my side, wrapping his hand around mine.

"Calm yourself, Maerilee," he whispers. "They are not here to hurt us."

I turn to him incredulously, and gesture toward their defensive poses, but he gestures toward our companions who've all taken a battle-ready stance. Then he gestures to my nearly invisible force-field, glittering vaguely in the sunlight.

As I look at the rebels' faces, I realize that they're looking to me in reverence rather than aggression.

25

THE END OF THE ROAD

Maerilee

My barrier hums around us, seemingly unnoticed by everyone but Permiton. He squeezes my hand, and the tension in my chest eases as I realize the barrier may not even be necessary. Permiton hasn't led us astray yet, and I know that he's seen something in the future that makes him confident the rebels aren't here to harm us.

I drop the barrier as a measure of good faith, my fears easing as Caelan steps forward, his sword sheathed, and drops to one knee. The other rebels follow suit, their heads bowed in reverence, their arms crossed over their chest in a sign of Altinnian allegiance. Tears spring to my eyes as I realize that Caelan didn't come to attack us. He's here to help us.

He looks up at me, his expression steady and filled with deep respect. "Princess Maerilee," he starts, his voice carrying a weight that quiets even the rustling trees around us. "I apologize for the misunderstanding. We haven't come to harm you. We've come to pledge ourselves to you and your cause."

Slowly, I watch as Akin, River, and Brook relax, dropping their defensive positions, though they still appear wary.

"You threatened us," River accuses.

"Ah," Caelan chuckles. "That was not meant to be a threat. I was simply expressing my sincere amazement that Bright Waters is real. I take it from your vials that your mission was a success?" His tone is earnest and friendly.

"It was," I affirm. "And now, if you'll excuse us, we need to get back to Altinna to save my mother."

His men are still bowed, waiting for his instruction to stand. They've surrounded us, so we really can't move on without them getting out of our way. But as I look at their faces, I realize they aren't looking at him. They're looking at me. They're waiting on my instructions.

"Rise, all of you," I command, my voice stronger than I expected. "Be at ease." Even Caelan falls in line, silently handing over his command to me

"Well, that was unexpected," Brook mutters behind me.

"We've come to warn you all," Caelan says, his face darkening. "The Oceanean army has been ordered to invade Altinna. Our scouts watched them board a ship to the border. We don't know the full extent of their plans, but my men and I stand ready to serve you."

For a moment, his words hang in the air, heavy and resonant. I glance at the others, each of them watching me closely, and I take a deep breath to steady myself. My heart is pounding, but I push the fear and uncertainty aside. There's no time for doubt now.

"How long ago did this happen?" I ask, panic gripping at me.

We're out of time. We knew the army would invade, but I didn't expect them to do it so soon. If we don't find a way to beat them there, all might be lost.

"They only left this morning," Caelan tells me, easing some of the tension in my chest. "We can still beat them if we leave now. My men know all of the best paths out of this kingdom. If we're swift, we can get to your castle before they invade and sound the alarm."

The weight of his words settles over me like a heavy cloak. My mother, my kingdom, my people are all at risk. In fact, it's my fault that this is happening. I look to River and Brook, the two brothers who've pledged their loyalty to me. The former sons of our greatest enemies. For a moment, I think perhaps I should have just chosen one of them and saved us all from this mess. But as I look between them, then to Akin and Permiton, I realize that I had no choice in the matter. Now, even if I wanted to, I wouldn't be able to live without any of them.

"We'll return to Altinna immediately," I say, my voice firm. "We have what we came for, and now we must use it to save my mother and repair the barrier. Caelan, I'm counting on you and your men to protect us on the journey back and get us there safely."

He bows his head again. "As you command, Your Highness."

I turn to the others, my gaze sweeping over each of them in turn. Akin stands tall and steady, his protective instincts as sharp as ever. Brook, quiet but resolute, nods subtly, his trust in me evident. Permiton's expression is sure, confident in the decision I'm making, and that brings me some level of relief. River's gaze meets mine, unspoken words flickering between us before he smirks faintly, the tension easing just a fraction.

"We're going home," I say, my voice steady. "Together. Akin, you and Caelan will lead the way. Caelan, Akin will act as my military proxy from here on out. Whatever he commands, that's what you do."

"Understood, Your Highness," Caelan obeys, and the two men salute.

Akin suddenly looks more relaxed than I've seen him in days, and I realize what a toll it was to leave the rebels in the first place. But he did it because he trusts me. All of these men have walked beside me into the unknown because they have faith in me and love me. Our journey may not be over, but I know with all my heart that as long as we are together, we can make it.

The rebels fall into formation around us, their presence both comforting and sobering. I re-erect the protective barrier, keeping it around us as we move. It hums faintly, more as a precaution than a necessity. If what Caelan says is true, I don't expect us to run into any of the Oceanean soldiers, but I'm not willing to risk it.

We keep a quick, grueling pace, pushing ourselves farther and faster than I would think possible. The rebels seem comfortable with this pace, as does Akin, but the rest of us struggle silently as we make our way out of the mountains, keeping to covered, forest paths.

Though my body is exhausted, my steps are firm, my mind resolute. Every step brings us closer to Altinna, to saving my mother, and to the fight we know is waiting for us. It might kill me to make it there, but if we slow down, I know there is no chance of us making it to Altinna before the army.

"At times like this, I wish we had wings," River laughs beside me, his amused tone a nice reprieve from the pace of the journey.

"I wonder how that works," I murmur thoughtfully, realizing I haven't put any thought into what a binding ceremony might look like.

In my kingdom, fae get their wings when they're bound to their One. I have no idea how a binding ceremony would work with the five of us, though. Would everyone get wings? Would any of us? I nearly burst out laughing at the thought, realizing that I've spent all this time with my Four without ever considering what would come next.

Permiton snickers beside us, and I realize that he knows the answer to our ridiculously timed query. Thinking about the logistics of our binding is certainly a nice distraction from the ache in my muscles.

"All will work out as it should," he says simply, leaving us all alone to our thoughts.

Eventually, I find myself walking beside Caelan. His demeanor is calm, his movements purposeful, and I can see why the rebels follow him so loyally. He glances at me as we navigate a rocky decline, his expression thoughtful.

"Your Highness," he begins, his tone measured, "I must admit, you've impressed me."

I raise an eyebrow, a small smile tugging at my lips despite myself. "Is that your way of saying you underestimated me?"

His lips twitch in what might be amusement. "Not at all," he backtracks, his cheeks coloring. "I've heard the stories of Altinna's royal family, but seeing a member firsthand is humbling. Especially since I've been away from Altinna for so long."

"Why did you leave, anyway?" I ask curiously.

He chuckles to himself, as if he's just heard a hilarious joke. "That's a story for another time," he answers cryptically. "But let's just say, I'm very happy to be going home."

"That's good to hear," I tell him honestly. "Because there's going to be a long fight ahead of us. We need as many loyalists as possible."

"I'm sure you underestimate the amount of people who would take up arms for you," he says as we finally reach even ground.

The weight of his words fills me with a strange mix of relief and responsibility. These people are counting on me, on all of us, and failure isn't an option. I glance back at my group, their faces a mix of determination and exhaustion, and I know they feel it too.

Away from the mountain, the rebels lead us through thick forests that supposedly run the long way around the massive lake. Though the lake cuts straight through the border of Oceana, Caelan assures us that these forests will get us there quicker.

The trees grow denser, the air heavier, as though the very land knows what's coming. Akin takes the lead, his sword drawn, his gaze sharp as he scouts the path ahead. River and Brook flank me, their movements in sync as if all tension between them has finally vanished. Permiton walks slightly behind, his presence steady and reassuring.

We pause briefly to rest and hydrate near a small clearing, the rebels fanning out to keep watch. I sit beside Akin, who hands me a water skin without a word. I take it gratefully, the cool liquid soothing my parched throat.

"How are you holding up?" he asks, his voice low.

"I'm tired," I admit, leaning back against a tree. "But we're so close. I can feel it."

He nods, his gaze sweeping the horizon. "We're going to make it," he assures me.

His confidence is a balm to my frayed nerves, and I find myself leaning into it, drawing strength from his steadiness.

"Thank you," I say softly, and he glances at me, his expression softening.

"For what?"

"For always being here. For always believing in me."

He smiles faintly, a rare, genuine expression that warms me despite the tension in the air. "I've loved you since the moment I met you," he whispers against my hair, and my heart lurches. "That love will never go away."

The moment of quiet is interrupted by Brook, who approaches with a small map in hand. "We should reach the border by nightfall," he says, his tone measured. "If we keep this pace."

I nod, standing and brushing the dirt from my clothes. "Then we don't stop until we're there."

The rest of the journey is a blur of movement and focus, the trees thinning as we approach Altinna's borders. The familiar sight of the kingdom's rolling hills fills me with a strange mix of relief and dread. We're home, but there's no telling how far behind the enemy is.

As we crest the final hill, the sight before us steals my breath. The Oceanean army stretches across the horizon, a sea of soldiers and banners that makes my heart pound. They're so close to the border, too close, and I know we have no time to waste.

Caelan steps forward, his expression grim as he surveys the scene. "Your Highness, your orders?"

I glance at him, then at the others, and take a deep breath. "We get the waters to my mother," I say firmly. "Whatever it takes."

The rebels fall into formation, their loyalty evident in every step they take. And as we descend the hill toward the battle waiting for us, I feel the weight of my people, my kingdom, my family pressing down on me.

But I won't falter.

With my Four by my side, I know that we will fight to the death if that's what it takes to save my kingdom.

167

Thank you for reading! Book 3, *The Crown*, is now available here.

ALSO BY SADIE WATERS

Chosen by the Princess: A Reverse Harem Romance,

Realm of the Chosen Book 1

Loved by the Princess: A Reverse Harem Romance,

Realm of the Chosen Book 2

Ruled by the Princess: A Reverse Harem Romance,

Realm of the Chosen Book 3

Realm of the Chosen: The Complete Series

Demon Seer: Ember's Flames Book 1

Demon Hunter: Ember's Flames Book 2

Demon Slayer: Ember's Flames Book 3

Queen of Winter

A Sketch Away from Perfect: The Art of Having it All Book 1

A Palette Full of Lovers: The Art of Having it All Book 2

Book Three coming soon!

The One: Four Fae for the Princess Book 1

The Quest: Four Fae for the Princess Book 2

The Crown: Four Fae for the Princess Book 3

Follow me on social media!

Instagram: https://www.instagram.com/sadiewaters/

Facebook: https://www.facebook.com/sadiewatersauthor

Twitter: https://twitter.com/SadieWatersBook

Bookbub: https://www.bookbub.com/authors/sadie-waters

www.ingramcontent.com/pod-product-compliance
Lightning Source LLC
Chambersburg PA
CBHW060326310726
48976CB00007B/2466